THE
BROOK
FLOWS ON

Nick's World - 1948

THE BROOK FLOWS ON

PETER HUBIN

Published by Up North Storytellers

THE BROOK FLOWS ON

PETER HUBIN

Published by: Up North Storytellers
N4880 Wind Rd., Spooner, WI 54801

Library of Congress Control No. 2013937230

ISBN NO. 978-0-615-79803-5

Printed in the United States of America
By: Documation, 1556 International Drive,
    Eau Claire, WI 54701

The year is 1948 and Nick is a fifteen-year-old freshman in
high school. He spent most of the summer camping and trout
fishing. He met Savannah and they became great friends.
Nick likes to write and this book is his diary about his world.
He also attempts to write stories which are part of his diary.
This is a coming-of-age story and it is fiction, but reflective
of how things were in Nick's world in 1948.

PREFACE

Nick is a fifteen-year-old boy living in Spooner, Wisconsin. It is 1948 and Nick is a freshman at the Spooner High School.

Earlier that summer he camped in the Beaver Brook Wild Life area for two months. His camp was in a grove of tall white pines on the bank of this beautiful stream. Early on, he meets Savannah, a tall red-headed trout fisherman and her family. They become very good friends. Nick meets other people including Earl, a severely wounded World War II veteran that Nick invites into his camp.

Shortly after breaking camp, freshman football practice starts. Nick has worked hard at getting in shape and he especially worked on his 'Crazy Legs' moves. Nick has several friends on the team and they get together to hunt, fish and other things.

During the football season, Nick receives some news that nearly devastates him. Day by day, he deals with the news. He visits Savannah at Antigo, Wisconsin and she was a big help in dealing with this news.

Football season ends and Nick tries out for the freshman basketball team. Practices are hard but Nick makes the team. After two games, the deer season starts and Nick and his dad hunt as much as Nick's fathers job allows them to. Nick saw several bucks but could not shoot any of them for a variety of reasons.

THE BROOK FLOWS ON

My name is Nick and I live with my mom and dad on High Street in Spooner, Wisconsin. I am 15 years old and am about ready to start my freshman year at Spooner High School. It is early August of 1948 and football practice has just started. Mr. Jones is the head freshmen coach but he is assisted by Mr. Patrito. We have nearly completed the first week of practice and I am finally not as stiff and sore as I was a couple of days ago. We do a lot of drills and calisthenics to get us into shape. We have practice twice a day and there are about thirty ninth- graders trying out for the freshmen team.

We do wind sprints every practice. These vary from ten yards to fifty yards and I am as fast as any of the other players. We also do 'up-downs' - lots of them - each practice. When the coach blows the whistle we all dive onto the ground. We immediately jump back up and run in place until the next whistle. We keep doing this for many minutes and, believe me, we get very tired. We are up to twenty 'up-downs' now and the coach adds one more each day. Coach Jones does these with us and we feel that if he can do them, so can we.

We have learned a few plays and I have been practicing at halfback. We have several good players, but we don't know much yet. Another halfback is Darrell, and he is just about as fast as I am, but he is heavier and is hard to tackle. My friends, Jim & Jed, are both out for the team also. They are both working out in the line. We walk home after practice together and we sure are sore but we talk about how practice went. We have lots more to learn but we feel pretty good about how we are doing so far.

I have thought about my two months camping by Beaver Brook. I sure wonder how I had the courage to camp out, all by myself, after dark in a huge forest. Thinking back at it now, it seems scary but I toughed it out and really enjoyed my contact with nature and meeting Savannah, Earl and the others. I wonder how things are going for them.

I wonder how the three foxes are getting along. I

would really like to see the family of saw-whet owls. I have a very strong urge to return to the campsite, the sluice dam and the beaver pond as well as the star of the show - the Brook. I can sit and watch the water flow by the hour. Running water certainly fascinates me. Is it alive? Does it have a spirit? It babbles - is it trying to tell me something? It is home to hundreds of organisms, insects, fish, snails, clams, worms and others, all living in this brook during high water, low water, and in winter all frozen up. The water comes bubbling out of dozens of springs beginning at a small lake and ending at the Yellow River. As the brook flows north, more and more springs add water so it is several feet wide when it joins the Yellow River after flowing four and one-half miles.

One thing has bugged me. As I follow the brook from the sluice dam to the beginning of the meadows, I have to cross a small stream about one foot wide. For whatever reason I never investigated where that water started from. This Sunday I am going to ride my bike, take my hip boots and go visit the places I just wrote about including, finding where the source of that water by the meadows is. I really want to see the foxes and the owls again.

Saturday we had only one practice in the morning. Near the end of practice, the coaches organized an offensive team and a defensive team. This was the first time we would actually run plays against a defense. Darrell and I were the halfbacks, Jim and Jed both played guards. Our plays were simple. Dive play straight ahead when the quarterback gives the ball to the halfback. We ran this to both sides. Darrell ran for a touchdown the first play from the left side. Next play I took the handoff and broke through and I ran for a touchdown. I needed to switch hands and stiff arm the safety. Boy it felt good to break free and score. Other players rotated in and I got a chance to play right defensive end for a few plays and got in on one tackle.

On the walk home, Jim, Jed and I were excited. Boy football was fun. Jed had a fat lip but both of these guys got right into blocking their man. Since we had the afternoon off we decided to go fishing below the dam. We dug worms but also took spinning rods and lures. Maybe we will catch a musky.

Early Sunday, August, 1948

Mom made a couple peanut butter sandwiches for me and I filled my canteen with water and headed for Beaver Brook on my bike. Dad is driving a train today or I would ask him to go with me. I have the sandwiches in a knapsack, hip boots over the handlebars of my bike and I got on Highway 53 and headed south. I took Wild Life Road and where this road crosses the railroad tracks is where I stash my bike in the weeds and hike down the track toward the campsite. It is a beautiful day, clear blue sky, temperature is very pleasant and I am really looking forward to the next few hours.

I come to the trail leading to the campsite and follow it to the grove of tall pines. Today they really smell piney which was a smell that permeated the campsite this summer. I stood and looked around remembering what went on there this summer - the tent location, the fire pit, Earl's tent location. I looked up in the tall pines for the saw-whet owl family. After several minutes of looking I concluded that they were not around. All at once, I heard the screechy-scratchy call which brought a smile to my face. It came from across the brook and seemed to come from a large white pine. I put on my boots and crossed the stream. As I approached the tree, I searched for the little owl. I got under the tree and looked up but had no luck. I began looking in other trees nearby and then I saw the little owl way out on the end of a lower limb of the big pine. I moved toward its position and finally I was about five feet from it and it just sat there, looking at me with partly closed eyes. It was a thrill to see the owl and I began to inch closer. Eventually I reached up and actually touched one of its claws. It just shuffled farther out on the limb. I sure wanted to hold the owl and pet it.

I went back to the campsite and headed south toward where the foxes lived this summer. As I neared the den I was aware of something to my right. It was one of the foxes. It was watching me and not running away. It was about twenty feet from me and just watched me. I softly spoke to it and it cocked its head. About now the other two foxes ran up and stood beside the first fox. I decided to sit down and take out a sandwich and see if they would be interested in a bite or two. I took a bite and then held out a small piece toward the foxes. No takers. I flicked the piece toward them and all three ran up and pounced on it. The lucky one gulped it down so I tossed another piece, closer this time. Same result and by now they were about six or seven feet from me. I held a piece on my hand and all three carefully sneaked toward my hand. Finally, one made a quick move and grabbed the bread from my hand. I gave them several more pieces of the sandwich and apparently they liked the peanut butter. In a few minutes they had inspected me to their satisfaction and they all laid down together and went to sleep. Apparently they were sleeping when I found them.

I am surprised that all three foxes are still near the den. They appear to be nearly full grown and I thought they may have left the den area to find their own territory. Maybe they will stay with the parents through the winter. Anyway, it was a big thrill to see them and have them come to me like they did. As I sat there my thoughts went back to the owl. Perhaps he called so I would find it. I wonder where the rest of the family is.

Finally I got up which woke the foxes. They unpiled and stretched but did not follow me. In fact, they ignored me as I went back toward the campsite.

I crossed the Beaver by the campsite and headed toward the beaver pond. My path took me through some aspen that beavers had logged. This was at least seventy-five yards from the pond. A long way for them to haul branches and a great distance from the safety of the pond. I guess they have eaten up the food closer to the pond. I saw some ducks but no sign of any beaver. I waded out along the sticks stuck in the pond. I reached the point where the top of my hip boots were just out of the water. I watched the pool and a cloud passed in front of the sun and it reduced glare enough that I could see down into the pool. I saw movement and then I made out a large fish swimming a few feet below the surface. I estimated it to be about twenty inches long and appeared to be a trout. I wondered if it was the one that gave a big thrash and escaped as I was about to net it. I could see several much smaller fish also but then the cloud passed beyond the sun and I could not see into the water.

I left the pond, crossed on the beaver dam and headed northwest toward the sluice dam. I crossed on one of the timbers and sat down on the edge of the west bank. The water was quite roiling here because of the four timbers crossing the stream. From time to time I would see the flash of a trout. There was some quiet water at the north end of this pool. I did see a large trout in the sixteen to seventeen inch range swim into view and paused for a few seconds and then it was gone.

I was very near the small stream that I came to investigate its origin. On the edge of the 'meadows' I came to this one foot wide stream flowing from the southwest. It was in a small trench with sides about two feet high. I started following the stream and within about one hundred feet I came to a small pool surrounded by tag alder shrubs, reeds and lily pads.

This pool was about forty feet in diameter and was mostly circular in shape. The south end of the pool seemed more open so I carefully walked around so I could get near this small open spot of water. I finally got as close as I could and took a tag alder leaf and rolled it up and flicked it out into this small opening in the pool. It barely landed when a huge trout came up and grabbed the rolled up leaf. Wow!! This trout must be six or seven pounds, at least, and maybe more. How did this fish get here. The pool was about a hundred feet from the Beaver. The small stream flowed in a crowded, trash filled stream bed. I don't think a fish could swim that hundred feet through all that trash. Perhaps in the spring when all the snow melted the level of the Beaver was high enough to flood that trench so trout could swim up to this little spring fed pool.

This huge fish was way too big for this small pool. I wondered if we could catch it and put it in Beaver Brook where it would have more room. I could ask my dad to help and we could try to catch the fish, net it and put it in the stream. Looking at the pool it was logical to try to catch this fish from where I was standing. I got busy and trimmed off some tag alder branches with my knife. I probed the pond and found it dropped off rapidly and appeared to be about eight feet deep. There was a small shelf right in front of me that allowed the water to be only about two feet deep. I eased into this and started pulling reeds and using a stick with a small broken branch. I used it to drag lily pads to me where I could pull some of them up and get them out of the water. We would need the pool to be free of all these things if we had any chance to catch and net this giant fish.

By this time it was late afternoon and I headed toward the railroad tracks by going straight west. My route took me near the tangle of trees that Joe Pachoe apparently spent part of a winter in. I have wondered what ever happened to Joe. Did he die? Is he still wandering? Did he recover and go back to civilization? Anyway, I really don't want to run into Joe or some other apparently not normal person. I reached the tracks and headed north. I retrieved my bike and followed the Wild Life Road to Highway 53 and then to home on High Street in Spooner.

When I got home, both Mom and Dad were there. I told them about the owl, the three foxes, seeing the big fish in the beaver pond and finally telling about the small spring hole with the giant trout in it. I told them what I would like to do to catch and net the trout and put it in Beaver Brook. Dad was very interested and did not have to work the next Sunday. We agreed to try to catch the big fish and began lining up what was needed. Dad thought a casting rod would be needed to keep the fish out of the weeds and lily pads. We needed to make an extension for our net so we could reach out several feet farther than we can without some extension.

Late Monday, August 1948

Two a day football practices continue and we are working hard. The coaches put together a defensive team. We played against our offense and we had six linemen, two linebackers and three defensive backs. I was working at defensive back and the coaches told us what to do on certain plays, what action by the offense will cause you to react a certain way. We scrimmaged for a few minutes but most of the practice time are drills such as trying to pull the football away from a running back, blocking each other, tackling each other, wind sprints and those blasted up-downs. Between practices, Mom took me up to school to get registered and get locker assignments. Jim and Jed were going to share a locker and I really did not have a preference so the office assigned me to share a locker with Joe, a new student that lives just south of Spooner. The office lady said Joe seemed like a nice boy and we should get along fine. I got my class schedule - citizenship, math, history, biology, phy. ed., study hall and forestry.

Football got more intense each day. We learned more plays on offense. We got more variations of the 6-2 defense, scrimmaged more and more. Still working at right halfback on offense and left defensive back on defense. We run passing drills both on offense and defense. It sounds like we will not pass much but we must be ready to do so.

Saturday, Mid-August, 1948

Today the freshman football team had a short scrimmage against some of the junior varsity team. We played defense first and the JV mostly ran the football and we held up well. They did break loose off left tackle and we could not stop them. I was in on two tackles and recovered a fumble. We went on offense and I started at right halfback. The first play was a handoff to Darrell and he broke free for about twenty yards. Next play was a sweep around the left end and I carried the ball. I got about fifteen yards. A few plays later, we faked to the fullback and I ran a pass route to my right. The quarterback takes a few steps to draw in the defensive end and then throws a pass to me. I caught it and headed up field. The defensive back made a try for me and I switched hands and cut to the left - stiff-armed him and got by. The safety was right there but I switched hands, made a cut to the right and stiff-armed him, too, and ran for a touchdown. Wow, our guys were excited. The coaches put other players in and everyone played some. At the end of practice, the coaches told us we were improving but they didn't let us off those miserable up-downs. They told us to enjoy the rest of the weekend.

Dad and I completed our plans for tomorrow. We would use a Mepps French spinner and hoped the fish would strike it. We also dug worms and got rigged up to use them if the spinner failed. Dad found a five foot piece of an old wooden hand rail and we securely wired it on to the handle of my net. Mom was asked if she wanted to go but she declined. She did make us take the camera and a tape measure. I had a difficult time sleeping that night.

The next morning we rolled out early, had breakfast and headed to the small spring pond. We parked the car and walked the railroad tracks to the spot I came out on the tracks last week. I had blazed this trail so we could follow it to the pool. The plan was that Dad would cast the Mepps and if he caught the fish, I would step into the water and get the net ready. We carefully sneaked to the south end of the pool and Dad cast out the Mepps. He had barely started cranking when the surface of the pond erupted as this big fish grabbed the Mepps spinner. Dad's rod bent as the fish went deep. Dad was able to keep the fish right in front of him and after about two or three minutes the fish began to tire and it came to the surface. I had gotten into the water and on the first try I netted this beauty. Boy it was heavy as I lifted it out of the water. We decided to take the fish to Beaver Brook before we tried to get the Mepps out of its mouth in case he slipped off, it would be in Beaver Brook.

We quickly carried the big fish in the net to a large

pool seventy-five yards downstream from where the small stream enters the Beaver. We put the fish in the water to let it get its strength back. In a few minutes, Dad got out his needle-nosed pliers and started removing the hook as I held the beauty with both hands right behind its gills with my thumbs on its neck. The hook came out easily and Dad measured it at twenty-five and one-half inches. He dug in his pocket and pulled out a small fish scale and we carefully weighed it at seven and three-quarters pounds. Next, Dad got out the camera and he took a picture of me holding this monster trout. At least it was a monster for this small pool and stream. I waded to where the water was above my knees and put the fish in and held my hands under it for several minutes until it recovered from its ordeal and slowly swam away.

Dad wondered if there were other trout in the little pond. We went back and tried the Mepps at least a dozen times and nothing happened. We rigged up the angle worms and tried for about half an hour and nothing happened. Granted, we stirred up the water pretty good catching the fish so any other fish would be alarmed and may not be willing to bite on anything. Maybe we could come back next weekend and try again.

The spots on the trout were about as big as my thumb nail. It appeared to be in good health and we wondered how old it was. Dad thought at least seven years old. Apparently it was able to find enough to eat in this small pond. We wondered if it will have to fight any other big fish to establish which fish ranks higher. Maybe its great size will automatically give it the highest rank. We thought we were helping the fish by freeing it from its small pool. Perhaps it will have a difficult time competing for food against the smaller, quicker trout. Then again it will probably catch and eat these trout. Anyway, Dad and I feel good that we were able to do what we did. Dad suggested that maybe we could catch a few trout and release them in the small spring pond. We could wait two or three years and try to catch them and maybe put them in the stream also. Interesting idea and the trout season closes at the end of September.

   We got home and told Mom all about our adventure. She is anxious to finish the roll of film in the camera and get it developed so she can see this huge fish. After supper I wrote a letter to Savannah and told her about football and my visit to the owl, foxes and fish at the beaver pond. The bulk of the letter told about the small spring pond and the huge trout. I do feel sorry that Savannah was not able to help catch the fish. I did promise to send her a copy of the picture when we get it.

Early Tuesday, August, 1948

   Two a day football practice resumed yesterday. We went over mistakes made in the scrimmage with the JVs. Coaches are looking for punters, punt return men, kickoff kickers and kickoff return men. We continue with drills and daily scrimmages against our teammates. Our first game is two weeks from today. We play on Tuesdays after school. We will scrimmage the Junior Varsity team on Saturday morning. School starts next Monday. There was a meeting for new students and I was asked to come to it as my locker partner Joe was a new student. The principal, Mr. Gold, talked and explained that the meeting was mostly to get the new students a little familiar with the building and a new locker partner.

   I met Joe. He seems like a great kid. He has a big smile, seems friendly and is good sized. He is very strong looking. We hit it off right away. We took our class schedules and looked for the rooms each class would be held in. Joe and his family moved here from Rockford, Illinois. His mom and dad grew up around Spooner and after they were married they moved to Rockford so his dad could work in a factory. One of their relatives had a farm just south of Spooner and wanted to sell it as they were getting elderly. Both of Joe's parents grew up on farms around Spooner and always wanted to have a farm of their own. Now they do.

   I asked Joe if he was going to go out for football. He

said he would like to but didn't know who to contact and he never talked to his parents about playing. I told Joe that Mr. Jones was the main freshmen coach and we could go and see if he is in the coaches office and he could explain things. Joe said, "Lets go." We found Mr. Jones and I introduced them to each other and Mr. Jones explained about the physical, equipment, insurance and practice schedule. He offered to give Joe a ride home and meet his mom and dad. Joe thought that was a good idea. Since we were finished with the meeting, Mr. Jones offered to give Joe a ride to his home right then.

The next day after practice I called Joe. His mom answered and said Joe was helping his dad but he would be coming in for lunch soon. I will have him call you. Joe called and I asked him, "How did it go with Mr. Jones and your mom and dad?" Joe said, "It went fine but Mom and Dad want another day to think it over." I told Joe, "I bet you would really enjoy football and I would really like you to be on the team with me and the other guys. If you want me to go with you to get gear and a physical, give me a call." Afternoon practice I got a good rap on my face, a bloody nose and fat lips. There were no broken or chipped teeth. I sure wish there could be some kind of guard on my helmet.

Saturday Scrimmage, August 1948

Saturday morning we scrimmaged the Junior Varsity football team. There were no kickoffs or punts, but two referees whistled violations. Our team did alright. We moved the ball on the ground and we scored two touchdowns. Darrell got one and I got the other one. On defense we gave up very few yards and no touchdowns. I played left defensive back and intercepted a pass. The coaches seemed pleased with our play. Friday after practice Joe called and said his mom and dad gave their approval to play. He rode his bike into school and I met him there along with Mr. Jones. An appointment was made for the doctor to give Joe a physical. After that he was fitted with gear and because Joe was late he didn't get the best fit on shoes and shoulder pads.

Late Monday, August, 1948

Last week of practice two times a day. Getting ready for our first game which is next week Tuesday, the day after Labor Day. Savannah called last night. Boy it was good to hear her voice. She is excited about starting high school at Antigo. Both schools start the Tuesday after Labor Day. She said she and her mom and dad would be at the cabin by Birchwood this weekend and invited my mom, dad and me to spend Sunday with them at the lake. Dad is working today but will be home tonight. I sure hope we can go. Mom and Dad are going to buy a 1949 Ford Custom car. Wow!! It has much different styling than our 1937 Ford and all the Ford cars built after World War II.

I went to the little spring hole where we caught the monster. No luck. I caught three brookies in the eight to nine inch range and quickly put them in the pool. Earlier, Dad told me to not fish that pond until I was graduated from high school. Those three fish could be two to four pounds by then if they survive.

Next day, Tuesday, August 1948

Dad got home and they would be happy to accept the invitation from the Casey's. I called Savannah to tell her the good news and asked what we could bring. She said, "The 'Brush Cop' and his family will be there too. Could your mom bring enough fried chicken for your family and ours and maybe a few bottles of soda?" A quick check with Mom and she said OK. I asked Savannah how to get to the cabin and she told me and I wrote it down. I am sure looking forward to seeing Savannah.

Practice is scrimmage everyday and some drills but we work on punting, punt blocking and trying to find someone that can snap the ball to our punter, Andy. We work on fielding punts and I am one of the punt return men. I am learning to make a fair catch signal and not catch the ball inside the ten yard line. We get a steady dose of the rules. There are plenty of them.

Joe has gotten his gear, his physical taken and has been working out doing wind sprints, calisthenics and up-downs. I really like Joe and hope he is interested in playing fullback. He won't be eligible for the first game but he may be able to practice with us on Thursday and Friday. I invited him to stop at my house after practice on Tuesday. I told him about getting in a stance before the ball is snapped to the quarterback. I explained the hole numbering. Right guard is 1, right tackle is 3, end is 5 and outside the end is 7. On the left side the left guard is 2, tackle 4, end is 6 and outside end is 8. The backs numbers are quarterback 1, right halfback is 2, fullback is 3, left halfback is 4. So a play called 21 is the right halfback running at the right guard. 34 is the fullback running at the left tackle. I showed Joe how to be sure your arm closest to the quarterback is raised so the ball can be put in your gut without a fumble. Once you have the ball hold on to it with both hands, one on each end. DON'T FUMBLE!! After you get the ball, run low and watch your blockers. Run behind their blocks. When the run has ended, go down. Don't let the other team strip the ball from you.

Next Day, Wednesday, August 1948

More scrimmages. We put in sweep plays to each side. If going right it is 47 and the right end blocks the defensive tackle, right tackle pulls and looks for a linebacker. I block the defensive end and one or both guards pull and team with the fullback to lead the play around the end. Same rules for 28 which is me carrying around the left end and Darrell blocks the end. That is the key block. Coach tells me to go straight at the end and block him at the knees, block through him. I am learning and can block our ends most of the time. It is a fun play to run and can be a big gainer. We are looking forward to playing the Barron freshman on our field next Tuesday. Jim and Jed are really doing a good job of blocking. We have named them 'Rough' and 'Tough'. Jed is 'Rough' and Jim is 'Tough'. We worked on kickoffs and coverage and kickoff returns. Darrell and I are the deep backs. On defense we work covering trick plays like the sleeper play, Statue of Liberty, cross country pass to the quarterback and others. If we are not sure we call a time out or tackle the football. Don't give up a big play on trickery. There sure is lots to learn. The coaches said we will work on defending trap plays, draw plays and screen passes Thursday and Friday.

Friday of Labor Day Weekend, September 1948

Afternoon practice (last one of the two practices per day). Hard practice, like game conditions. Kick offs, punts, and the clock was used to tell quarters and half. Players were assigned to various teams - kickoff, kick return, punt, punt return as well as the offensive team and the defensive team. The coaches really gave us a pep talk. First game for all of us and we need to concentrate on our responsibilities and take it serious!

A surprise to us is that our game jerseys will be handed out after practice. Since there is a home varsity game tonight with Frederic we should try to come to the game and wear our game jersey. We did our up-downs and headed to the showers. Coaches called us in and gave us a red jersey. My number is 37. We are all getting excited about our game with Barron next Tuesday.

Joe worked out with us on Thursday and today. He got to play some defense at linebacker and looked pretty good. I asked him to stop at my house on the way home on his bike. He did stop and we talked about football and about his family. He has a younger brother and a younger sister - sixth and fourth grades. His mom just got a job at the Bank of Spooner and will start next Tuesday. His dad is a carpenter and has the farm also. The farm is just south of Spooner right where the two railroad lines join up. That is just a short distance from where I ran when I took Margaret into Spooner after she had been hurt falling into Beaver Brook. Joe said, "We have ten cows, some pigs and chickens and a big garden." He also said, "I have to help put up hay tomorrow." I asked, "Do you think they need any help?" He said, "I don't know as we have not put up hay on this farm yet. If you want to come in the afternoon we may need the help." I asked him to come back to my house by 6:30 and we will meet up with 'Rough' and 'Tough' and go to the game. He thought he should be able to do that. Then it occurred to us that it would be dark by the time the game got finished so maybe he could stay over night with me. He will ask his mom and dad.

Saturday of Labor Day Weekend, September 1948

Joe spent the night and went home after breakfast. Mom and Dad sure like him. The varsity beat Frederic last night 19-7. Joe and I met 'Rough' and 'Tough' and we hung around together and met lots of our teammates. We were all proud to be wearing our red football jerseys. We did see a few girls. Joe seems to attract lots of interest from them.

After lunch I rode my bike to Joe's place. He and his dad were getting ready to start putting up the hay. Several days earlier, Joe's dad cut the hay and it was dry now. This morning he raked it into windrows that went around and around the field. They were just hooking up the tractor to the hay wagon when I got there. Next they hooked a thing called a hay loader to the back of the wagon. Then they went to the hayfield and straddled the windrow with the tractor and wagon. Joe's brother, David drove the tractor. As they moved forward, the hay loader picked up the hay and pushed it up the hay loader until it fell onto the hay wagon. Before this happened, they put rope slings down and the hay was piled on the rope, when the proper amount of hay was loaded, the tractor stopped and they put down a second rope sling. They started up and added more hay and distributed it so it made an even load. My job was to tramp, or pack, the hay down so it didn't take up so much space. Finally, Joe's dad called "whoa" and David stopped the tractor. Joe climbed down on the frame of the front of the wagon. He unhooked the hay loader and climbed on the tractor with David and they headed to the barn.

The big door on the front of the barn had been opened and that is where David drove toward. He pulled up close to the barn and at the right time, his dad told him to stop. Joe unhooked the wagon and David drove it to the back of the barn. Joe put a ladder up against the load of hay and we could climb down. Joe's dad pulled on the trip rope and pulled the carrier out to the end of the track. He continued pulling and the pulley that the slings will be attached to finally reached the top of the load. The end of the slings were found and attached to the pulleys that will be pulled up to the carrier. Finally, the slings are attached, everyone is off the load and the signal to begin pulling is given. The big hay rope pulls the pulleys together and finally the huge sling full of hay is pulled up higher and higher until it reaches the carrier. When the pulleys contact the carrier the entire load is pulled into the barn. When it gets to the desired location, the trip rope is pulled and then one end of the sling disconnects and the hay drops to the floor of the haymow with a mighty crash. The big hay rope is unhitched from the tractor and the whole process is repeated and the second sling full of hay is in the haymow. We hook up to the wagon and head out to the hay loader to load another wagon full of hay.

After two more loads we all took hayforks and went into the haymow to mow the hay off to the sides of the barn. The haymow is huge and I guess it has to be in order to get enough hay for the winter time stored in there. Now this job really sucks! First you climb up on these mounds of hay and then fork it off to the sides in order to make room for more hay. Not only is it hard to do but the haymow is hot. We got those three loads spread out so we are getting ready to head out for another load, but Joes' mom comes out with a big pitcher of Kool-Aid and a tray of cookies. We all retire to the shade under a tree and take a break. Even Joe's sister, Sarah, comes out to take a break with us. She is a cute kid and really is giving David a hard time about his tractor driving.

Finally all the hay is in the barn and it is time to milk the cows. Joe and I go to the pasture to round them up and get them into the barn. About now I decide that I better go home. I say good-bye to everyone and they all thanked me for helping, including Sarah. That sure seems like a nice family - I hope Joe and I can become good friends. I have not asked Joe but I bet he is a very good student. It sure looks like he gets lots of support from his mom and dad, similar to the way my mom and dad support me. This was a fun day.

Sunday of Labor Day Weekend, September 1948

Mom has her fried chicken all ready and Dad has a case of pop in several flavors. We get in the new 1949 Ford Custom 4-door car painted with Henry Ford's favorite color of paint - black. We head to Savannah's cabin. I really am anxious to see Savannah - her parents also. It should be a fun day. Mom got the roll of film developed and we have several pictures of the huge trout to show everyone. On the way, I asked Dad if he thought we had broken any fishing laws when we caught the big fish and put it in Beaver Brook. I told him that since Savannah's uncle is a game warden, I don't want him to pinch us if we did something illegal. Dad did not know of any law or rule that we may have violated but he also said, "Ignorance of the law is no excuse." Maybe when we get there we can ask Mr. & Mrs. Casey if they know of any reason we could not release the trout into Beaver Brook even if we caught it in a spring hole a few feet away. We followed Savannah's directions and drove right to the cabin and there she was. I jumped out and ran to Savannah and gave her a big hug. Boy, she is pretty.

Elon and Kathy Casey came out and welcomed us. Both sets of parents seem to really get along fine. The fried chicken sure smelled good on the trip here. It was taken into the cabin as was the soda. Savannah wanted to see the picture of the trout. Elon and Kathy crowded around as Mom got the pictures out of her purse. All three were amazed at the size of the trout. It was twenty-five and one-half inches long and weighed seven and three-quarters pounds. Dad told about how the trout was caught, carried to Beaver Brook and released all within about five minutes. The trout was only out of the water about one minute. We gave it time to recover and the big fish swam away into deep water. We went back a week later and fished the spring pond and caught nothing. We wondered if it got in during a time of flooding and once the water level went down it could not get back to the stream. Also, someone could have put the trout there. "Now, we have a question for all three of you. Did we break any fishing regulations when we released the trout into Beaver Brook, about seventy-five feet away from the spring pond?" Dad asked. "Water does flow out of the spring pond and into Beaver Brook all the time. It is a small stream but definitely is a tributary of Beaver Brook." Dad continued, "Nick had wondered if we should tell the 'Brush Cop' about the fish." Elon said, "Since the pond is a tributary of Beaver Brook it would be considered part of Beaver Brook. A case somewhat similar happened in Langlade County a few years ago. Two men were fishing a spring pond on private property with no permission. Wardens observed them catching several trout and finally moved in to apprehend the culprits." Elon continued, "The perpetrators were too quick for the wardens and ran to a nearby stream and threw the trout into the stream. The wardens arrested the two and took them to a judge. The wardens argued that the men took the fish from one body of water and put them in another. The judge asked if the spring pond had an outlet into the stream. The wardens said it did and the judge ruled that the fish had just been transported to another part of the same stream. That is legal and since there was no evidence that charge was dropped but the trespassing charge stood." Elon said, "The 'Brush Cop' is the one who told me about the case, so I think you would have not broken any fishing regulations and you could tell anyone you wanted about your rescue mission."

After all had a look at the pictures, Elon said he had a spring pond story to tell. He said, "Around Antigo there are many spring ponds. My boss, Morgan, Superintendent of Antigo Schools and Mike, who was the director of the Antigo Vocational School on the same block as the high school, were real trout fishermen. They tied their own flies, used light weight tackle with tapered leaders down to one and one-half pounds. They fished spring ponds exclusively. One day they were in their flat bottomed boat on a spring pond and Mike had on a number 22 ant which is about one-eighth of an inch." Elon continued, "Early on Mike got a fish on the fly. He could tell it was big and for two hours he never saw the fish. Finally it came up and both could see it and it was huge. Forty-five minutes later, Morgan was able to net this giant and get it into the boat where the hook promptly fell out of its mouth. This giant was a female brown trout that weighed ten pounds. This fish hangs on the wall of a bar in downtown Antigo to this day."

Savannah and I went down by the lake to be by ourselves for awhile. She wanted to know all about how my football playing had gone. She wished she could see me play. She was impressed that I had gotten to know Joe and had helped to get him familiar with school, rooms and everything and I had also encouraged him to try out for football. She listened to my tale of helping put up hay yesterday and she thought that was wonderful. Savannah had been assigned a new student to help her with her locker, finding all the classrooms and help her become familiar with Antigo High School. This is a school about three times the size of Spooner and even though Savannah went to the Antigo Junior high on the same block as the high school, there were things about the high school that she had to learn too. The student Savannah helped went to one of the rural schools in the district so she was not completely new like someone just moving into the district. Antigo and Spooner are among the very largest districts in the state by area. Each have many school buses with long routes. Many students ride an hour in the morning and an hour after school to get home. That is what both of us heard at the meeting to help new students. Savannah has been practicing her clarinet in hopes of making the varsity band. She would be thrilled if that would happen. Seven clarinetists graduated from last years band and of the freshman clarinet players that she knows about, she thinks she might be in the top four. There might be some clarinet players coming in from the rural school as all these schools have music programs, too. Anyway, Savannah really wants to be in the varsity band.

Savannah's classes will be very similar to mine - civics, English, history, math, home economics, study hall and physical education. She is trying to find out as much as she can about the teachers she will have. Her dad gives her very little help here because it would not be fair to other students unless he could tell them also. No amount of pleading did any good. All he did say was, "After looking at your class schedule and who your teachers are, I would say you will have very good, dedicated teachers." Savannah also plans to try out for the chorus but is more interested in the varsity band. If she is in either band or chorus, they would meet during her study hall period. That means more homework at night.

Savannah's mom advised her and she has a new wardrobe of clothes for school. She has three close friends that are all freshman and live within a block or two of Savannah. They have many classes together and will walk to and from school together. Savannah says they 'gossip a lot'. She says the others are jealous because she has this mysterious male friend in a far away town. Apparently, talk about boys dominates most of their conversations. All of these girls are in band and no one else plays the clarinet. All are hoping to make the varsity band but really don't think they will make it. A couple of these girls have friends on the Antigo freshmen football team and they will have their first game next week also. It will be against Merrill and will be at Antigo. Savannah says Antigo is in the Wisconsin Valley Conference with Rhinelander, Merrill, Wausau, Stevens Point, Wisconsin Rapids and Marshfield.

About this time, the 'Brush Cop' and his family arrived. We went to the cabin to meet them. The three girls, Mary, Helen and Beth seemed happy to see us and wanted to know if we could have another basketball game, provided I didn't fall in the briar patch again.

Elon pulled out the picture of me holding the huge trout. The 'Brush Cop' claimed it was the biggest trout he had ever seen coming from the waters in this part of the state. He was very interested in how we caught it, what bait and then he asked, "Was it good eating?" We explained that we released it in Beaver Brook, about seventy-five feet from the spring pond. "You mean you did not release it back in the spring pond?" His voice took on a sinister tone and he looked right at me and said, "Nick, did you release that fish in Beaver Brook?" I was completely taken aback and started to mumble that, "Yes, I did." About then everyone standing there had dumbfounded looks on their faces. The 'Brush Cop' said, "That is too bad because it can only be released in the same waters. I am going to have to arrest you." I must have looked as white as a sheet but then he said, "I have no jurisdiction in Washburn County on the Sunday before Labor Day. You are off the hook." With that he had a huge grin on his face and came over to me and gave me a big hug. "Had you going for a while didn't I?" By this time my heartbeat began to return to normal as everyone had a big laugh, including me. The 'Brush Cop' said, "What you and your dad did was perfectly legal and a wonderful thing to do for that huge trout. You released it from its prison and I hope I didn't scare you too bad, but I could not resist the temptation." I realized that this tough game warden had a humorous side to him.

It was time for lunch so we all loaded our plates and began to chow down. During lunch Elon asked Savannah, "Do you remember where the old house was on the far side of Grandpa and Grandma's farm?" Savannah said she remembered it and thinks she could find it. Elon said, "You take the old road from across the road at the end of the driveway and follow it for about a quarter mile until you come to a small field. Look to your right and you will see the house back in a grove of trees. It was built about 1895 and the folks lived there until the 1920s when someone died of scarlet fever. The family approached Grandpa and Grandma about buying the land and buildings from them. They finally agreed on a price so it became part of their farm. Grandpa took the barn down and used the lumber to build a barn at his place. Nothing was ever done with the house. Apparently people thought the spirit of the dead person, a man, roams around in the house." Elon continued, "I don't believe there were any ghosts in the house."

Elon went on to say, "Kathy and I have been to the house several times before Savannah was born. It is a well built house in the New England cottage style with a wrap-around porch on three sides. Maybe after lunch Savannah could take Nick and the three girls for a hike to see the house." The girls chimed in with yah, yah - let's go. So as soon as we finished eating, off we went.

We followed the old road which was a nearly overgrown trail. It ran through a nice stand of oaks, basswood, ash and some aspen. It was well cared for as Grandpa did a good job of harvesting logs and selling some, and getting others sawed into lumber for use around the farm. We scared up six partridge, or ruffed grouse, and they returned the favor by scaring us too. Their being called 'thunderbirds' is certainly appropriate.

We arrived at the field and found lots of goldenrod growing around the edge of the field. They were in full bloom and looked just like their name - golden rods.

We approached the house and one of the girls said, "Boy, it sure needs paint." We got up to the house and were pleased with the style of the house. The wrap-around porch was neat. We decided to walk up on the porch which was three steps off the ground. All the windows appeared to be intact but the front door was open. We walked around three sides of the house by walking on the porch. We looked in through the windows and saw a living room with an old sofa in it. We saw a bedroom with an old bed and a spring through another window. The door opened into the kitchen and there was a sink, several cupboards, two chairs and several plates piled up on a countertop by the sink. A hand water pump was by the sink and we wondered if it still worked.

We could not resist the temptation to walk through the open door. All the girls insisted that I go first. I did, very carefully. I don't mind telling you that I was apprehensive but I slowly went in, with all four girls close behind. Someone said, "What was that noise?" We all said, "We didn't hear anything." Next, we went into the living room and saw that a stairway went up to whatever rooms were upstairs. Because of the style of the house, I figured that the rooms must have had low ceilings and could not be very large. They were probably bedrooms. We left the living room and went back into the kitchen where Helen noticed a trap door in the floor close to the back of that room. "We are not opening that door," said Helen. "That is where the ghosts are." We all agreed that we definitely would not open that trap door. We went into the bedroom and found a closet with a door on the back wall and it was closed. Mary said, "We are not opening that door - it looks creepy." I said, "I wonder what kind of room is behind that door. I know that I am not going to open it."

We went back into the living room. Savannah wondered, "Who were these people? Did they have kids like us? Where did they come from? Where did they move to?" Beth said, "We haven't seen any toys. Maybe they are upstairs. Lets go up and look." We reluctantly started up the stairs with me in the lead. Mary said, "What was that?" We all heard something that sounded like a footstep in one of the rooms upstairs. We all were on the stairs and I was two steps away from stepping on the floor then but we all were stopped. Listening and wondering what we heard. All at once, there was a crashing sound like something falling to the floor behind the closed door to one of the rooms. We didn't hesitate - WE RAN!!!! Down the stairs into the living room, and into the kitchen. About now there was another crash coming from upstairs. We ran faster. No one bothered with the three steps down. We jumped. Savannah took Helens hand and I picked Beth up and we ran. Mary could keep up pretty well. Finally we reached the trail leading back to the cabin. We stopped to catch our breath. The three small girls were wide eyed and puffing from running. After a minute or so, we all started laughing, mostly at ourselves for being so afraid. What made those sounds? Is someone in that house? Could it be some animal? Maybe the house is falling apart. We did not see anything but we all agreed that we definitely heard something and it really scared all of us. No one wanted to bring up the idea of ghosts but I really think we all wondered if it could be a ghost.

As we walked back to the cabin, we all looked back over our shoulder from time to time. When we reached the cabin the three mothers were sitting in the sun by the cabin. Beth and Helen proceeded to tell the ladies what they had heard at the house. The mothers listened intently and asked some questions. They were thankful that everyone was safe and even got a chuckle after hearing how scared we all were. Dad and the 'Brush Cop' had gone fishing. Elon had gone to help Grandpa with a job he needed help with.

After resting up and rewarding ourselves with a bottle of pop, the girls wanted to play a game of basketball, so we did. Mary and I played Savannah and Helen and just like the game in July, we got beat but it was a close game. By this time it was mid-afternoon and Savannah and I went down by the lake and sat on the chairs there. Savannah asked me what I thought about what we heard in the house. I wondered if someone was in the house, or did we trigger something to fall as we went upstairs. Maybe it was like a booby trap but not rigged up to hurt us but to scare us good. Savannah agreed that maybe someone had rigged up those stairs so if we stepped on a certain step it was rigged to produce the sound like someone's footstep. If we continued on maybe stepping on another step caused something to fall over with a crash. Who would do something like that? Is there something behind those closed doors that someone did not want us to see? That trap door in the kitchen is real creepy. Savannah said that she has read that people had a small basement under the house to store things like potatoes, carrots, rutabagas, etc. Maybe that is what is under the trap door in that house. Whatever the reasons are, I don't think any of the five of us are ever going back in that house.

I took Savannah's hand and there was instant electricity between us. We took a little walk along the lakeshore and came to a dense clump of Arbor Vitae. We ducked into this clump and I pulled Savannah to me and we kissed. It was a nice long kiss as we hugged each other. We kissed again and this time Savannah reached behind her back and took one of my hands and put it on her left hip. WOW! We continued our embrace and we snuggled closer, maybe closer than we had ever been. Finally, we separated, somewhat red faced but having really enjoyed our few minutes alone in the Arbor Vitae. My heart was really beating for the second time today. Emotions are powerful. I realize that I have strong feeling for Savannah. I think she also has strong feeling for me. We have to work very hard to keep our emotions at a manageable level when we are together. That is difficult.

The afternoon is done and food began to be prepared. Hamburgers on the stove in the cabin and hot dogs over the fire built by the lake. Dad and the 'Brush Cop' caught six bass which were filleted and split between the three families. All would have a fish meal sometime soon.

We sat around the fire, ate and then stayed in our chairs and visited. The three young girls retold the adventure in the old house at the urging of Elon, since he had not heard the story immediately after it happened. The girls were enthusiastic in the re-telling of this afternoon. Elon wondered what could have made these scary sounds. Ah-ha! As we sat there something made me wonder if Elon knew more about those sounds than he is letting on. He was supposed to be helping Grandpa with a job that needed his help - or was he? I don't think Elon was in the house because he was still at the cabin when we left to go to the old house. Perhaps he could go to the house by a different route and have arrived at the house slightly after we went into the house. What if he had gone to the house earlier and rigged up things that could be tipped over by pulling on a string or cord from outside the house, well out of sight from us. Also, the front door was open but there was no evidence of small animals, like raccoons getting into the house. Grandpa would have a ball of twine around his farm and with some work ahead to time, someone could really play a prank on the five of us. We were completely fooled. I don't have any proof but I am suspicious that if we went back to the house we may find evidence to support this theory, then again maybe all the evidence had been removed after a big laugh was had at our expense.

I looked at Elon, long and hard. Oh, yeah, he is capable of pulling off a trick like that. My hat is off to him and I don't plan to ever confront him about evidence or anything. Then a thought crossed my mind. When we left the house in a big hurry, we did not close the front door. If Savannah and I walked over near the house we could see if the front door was open or closed. I suggested to her that we go for a walk toward the house and she agreed so off we went. We did not have much time because we had to return to Spooner soon as Dad had to go to work very early tomorrow. We got near the house and sure - THE DOOR WAS CLOSED. Case closed, Sherlock.

I don't ever plan to tell Savannah about my theory. She is a bright girl, maybe she will arrive at the same conclusion as I did. Apparently there is more to Elon than meets the eye.

Savannah and I head back to the cabin and I brought up the fact that Spooner teachers have a convention and we won't have any school on Thursday and Friday, October 6th - October 7th. My football game will be on Thursday and there won't be any practice until the following Monday. I wondered if I could come to Antigo and visit, maybe on Friday. Savannah said, "That would be wonderful. I just noticed the football schedule and I remember that the Red Robins play the Rhinelander Hodags on Friday, October

7th - at Antigo. This is about the biggest game of the year because these teams play for the 'Bell' which the winner gets to keep until the next Antigo-Rhinelander game. It has been going on for about fifty years. Many people bring bells to the game, sleigh bells, classroom bells, little bells, and big school bells. Hundreds of bells are there and it is a fun time. You need to go very early to get a seat in the stadium."

I told her that I could take a train or bus and I would have to check on that. "Do you think your folks would mind if I visited your mom, dad and you?" Savannah said, "I am sure they would be happy to have you visit and I am sure you could stay with us. Boy, will my girlfriends be anxious to see you." If that could all be worked out it would be a fun time. Savannah and I stopped on our way back to the cabin. We hugged and kissed for several minutes and finally decided that we needed to get back. We held hands as we walked. I could have hugged and kissed much longer but we have got to control our emotions and that is getting more and more difficult. We said goodbye to everyone and thanked everyone for a wonderful day. The three little girls came up and gave me a hug. They do seem like very nice kids. I hope they don't have nightmares about the noises in the old house. We drove to Spooner and I spent two hours writing up the events of today. Good night.

Monday of Labor Day Weekend, September, 1948

Dad is driving his train today and Mom has only a couple small tasks that require my help. Once they were done I decided to attempt to write a story. It will be called **The Mob and the Deer Hunter** (I think).

Ted was a young man, 28 years old and was married to Ann, also 28 years old. They had a four-year- old boy named Jake and a two-year-old daughter named Lois. They lived on a small farm a few miles east of Spooner, Wisconsin. The year was 1934. The depression was affecting everyone's life including Ted and Ann. Ted worked in a factory in

Milwaukee and was laid off in 1932. Ann had an uncle at Spooner and he knew of this small farm that was for sale. If they could buy the property, her uncle would help them buy livestock and machinery. Ted had been in the army and when he got discharged he received a fair-sized check that he had never cashed. It was enough to make a down payment on this 70 acre farm with some money left over. There was a small house with no running water, but it was large enough for the four of them. There was a well and water was pumped to the milk house and stored in a tank raised about two and one-half feet above the floor of the milk-house. The water ran by gravity to water the cows, pigs and chickens. There was a ten gallon water heater that produced hot water. If some hot water was taken out, more water was drained from the big tank and put in the water heater to replace the hot water used.

There was a barn to store hay and it could hold about ten cows in stanchions. There were three small pens for calves. There was a brooder house for chickens and a building for pigs. Another building was a corn crib, oats granary and one side was a small garage.

Life was hard for Ted and Ann and for the kids. Many, many people could not pay their property tax and the land reverted to whoever had loaned money to buy the property. Land that was owned free and clear could still be lost if the property tax could not be paid. That land reverted to the county. Several large lumber companies had logged the timber off but still owned the land. Much of that land became county forest land when taxes could not be paid. Ted and Ann's property was right next to a large tract of county forest land. This land was open to the public to hunt and fish.

Ted was a good hunter and he shot rabbits, squirrels, duck, partridge and deer. Ted and Ann both fished in the lakes nearby and many meals of fish were caught. A large garden, strawberry beds and raspberry patches produced food for the family and some of the produce was sold. The cows produced milk and income as the milk was sold. Pigs and chickens were butchered for meat. Eggs were eaten, but many were traded for what groceries were needed from the grocery stores in Spooner.

Ted really looked forward to the deer season in Wisconsin. It opened on November 19, 1934. Not only did the family need the meat, it was a real challenge to hunt these bucks. Ted was a very good shot with his lever action .38-55. The gun was his dads but an injury made hunting impossible so Ted's dad gave the gun to him several years ago.

Before the season opened, Ted purchased his deer license which included a back tag that had to be displayed on his back with an appropriate amount of red clothing so other hunters could see him. Ted had eleven .38-55 cartridges and thought that would be enough. He had shot a buck in each of the past two years and only used one shot for each deer.

Opening morning means getting up at four o'clock in the morning to milk the cows, take care of the pigs and chickens, clean the barn, carry water and do whatever chores are required.

Finally, Ted comes in the house, now nice and warm from the wood fire in the wood burner in the front room plus heat from the wood cook stove. Breakfast is eaten with the family and Jake really wants to go along. Ted puts on warm hunting clothes, boots, cap and gloves. This year he bought a light weight red windbreaker to put on over his wool jacket. He stuffed sandwiches in his pocket. His back tag is pinned in the center of the windbreaker which has a hood. Ted left the house at 6:30 a.m. with just a tiny hint of light in the eastern sky. The temperature was about 20° F., with a light breeze from the southwest. Early yesterday it snowed about four inches which Ted thought was about perfect. It is easier to see dark deer, easier to follow a wounded deer and the snow made walking quieter.

Ted moved straight south from his buildings. He crossed his fence and was now on private property, but no one ever came around so Ted hunted on this land even though he was not sure where the property boundaries were.

By the time he had walked this far it was somewhat lighter and close to the legal shooting time. He heard a couple distant shots and thought, "That's the first of dozens I will hear today."

Ted's way of hunting is to move slowly, quietly and stop for some time on small hilltops, rises or any spot that gave him a good view, hopefully in all directions.

One goal Ted had was to be able to see a deer lying in its bed and be able to shoot it there. Deer are very alert to any sound or motion and it is very hard to sneak up on them. Windy weather helps the hunter if they hunt into the wind and because the wind is blowing branches, leaves on branches and trees swaying makes it harder to spot a hunter moving but it also makes the deer nervous. Anyway, Ted is like most hunters that find shooting a buck takes a lot of luck even if their skill level is high.

By mid-morning, Ted has gone about three-eighths of a mile from his property. He saw two deer at a distance for about three seconds. Shooting has not been heavy. The wind had switched and was now out of the southwest and the temperature was rising and he guessed it was close to 30° F. So far he had not seen any hunters or hunters tracks. This is prime deer country and since it is public land there are lots of hunters. The one drawback is that he is already about five-eighths of a mile from Highway 70 and that is a long way to pull a deer, plus it is a long walk with heavy clothes just to get back this far. Many hunters go back farther than that.

Ted now hunted toward the east, toward some high hills and big ridges. There are lots of oak trees on these ridges and deer really like white oak acorns and will show up in late afternoon to dig for them in the snow.

On this course Ted has set, he will go past a homestead that got turned over to the county two years ago for delinquent taxes. Ted knew the people and shared some work with them. Their name was Miller and they moved to Rice Lake, Wisconsin. Bruce was one of their sons and he lives in Rice Lake, too. He still comes up to his old farm to hunt. Ted expects that he is hunting near there today. Other years he has started a fire in the house which is still standing. None of the buildings have been torn down. The county probably has hundreds of properties like this and just doesn't have the manpower to take the buildings down.

Ted sees the buildings and sees smoke coming from the chimney of the house. Bruce must be around someplace. By now it is early afternoon and Ted swings more toward the north and is heading for a very high ridge that forms a circular ridge for a very deep, steep sided valley. It is as if something started digging into the side of a hill and kept digging in farther and farther until it dug more than halfway into the hill. The hill kept sliding down into the hole. The digging stopped, leaving the steep walls and eventually trees grew on it. One thing about this formation, a hunter either hunts up on the ridge or down at the bottom. No hunting on the steep walls. Deer, however have made trails following the contour of the ridge so a person looking down from the ridge may see deer on these trails below.

By 2:30 p.m. Ted was cautiously approaching the top of the ridge and would soon be able to see down to the bottom of the valley. Finally, he could see all the way down to the bottom. His eyes swept the entire view in front of him, looking for the familiar brown of a deer either standing, lying down or moving. Something caught his eye. Down at the bottom of this valley, a little to the northwest, he could see some hunters moving in his direction. There appeared to be three hunters and Ted watched them for about ten minutes. The hunters stopped and two of them pulled away a few feet from the third man. All at once they raised their guns and shot the third man! This man immediately fell to the ground and lay still. Holy Cow! I just witnessed a murder.

He thought he better get off that ridge before they start shooting at him. He didn't think they had seen him at that point. He was just turning to his right to start back tracking when he felt something hit his left shoulder. Then he heard the shot. He had been shot. The shot seemed to come from his right so he looked in that direction as he ran for any cover before more shots were fired. Another shot rang out and hit the tree he had stopped behind. Now he could see a man standing by a tree and getting ready to shoot again. His shoulder was beginning to hurt really bad and it was bleeding and the blood was dripping on the snow. His arm just hung there as he could not raise it. He was trapped behind this tree which was quite large. The shooter was about seventy-five yards away. Ted realized that he needed to make a run for it but his level of pain was very high and he felt faint. Would he be able to run? He carefully looked around the tree and the shooter seemed to be in the same place. He immediately fired a shot that tore a chunk of bark off where Ted's face was just a moment ago. This guy must be a very good shot.

Ted looked for a path going off the ridge toward the southwest. He wanted to stay near as many trees as possible. If he could run at least fifty yards and then find a place to shoot from, it might draw the man out if he thought Ted was getting away. By now his shoulder was really throbbing. He saw a hummock about fifty yards away. A hummock is caused when a large tree is blown over and brings up a big gob of dirt in its roots. When the roots rot away there is a pile of dirt and a hole where the dirt came from. Ted would head for the hummock and once there, he would try to get a shot at this guy, that is if he can make his left arm work enough to shoot with his right shoulder.

Ted took a breath and took off. Immediately, there was a shot and another and another. He reached the hummock and hunkered down as low as he could behind the small hill. He looked to where he thought the shooter was and got his rifle up and resting on his left arm. He could raise his arm a little. Ted saw the shooter and he was coming after him. He cocked the .38-55 and looked for an open shot. All at once, there was an opportunity. Ted aimed and fired and he hit the man. Ted thought it was in the chest area. The man immediately went down and was moving around like he was in pain. Ted put another round in the chamber and aimed at his legs. That shot also was on target. The shooter seemed out of commission at this time so Ted started walking as fast as he could toward the southeast.

By now it was about 4:00 p.m. and the sun was very low in the southwest. When Ted had gone about one- hundred yards he came to a log that he could sit on. Ted brushed the snow away, sat down and tried to figure things out. He looked at the wound on his left shoulder. It had missed any bones. The bullet hit near the point of his shoulder and had gone straight through. It made a large hole where it came out and it was bleeding very steadily. The bullet had made a hole in his windbreaker and jacket and he had a difficult time seeing the back of the wound where the bleeding was the worst. Ted needed to stop the bleeding but what could he use? His handkerchief, but it was not clean. Finally he thought about his undershirt. He ripped off a portion of it, rolled it up and pushed it into the backside of the wound. He did take out his handkerchief and ripped the hem off all four sides and tied them together to make a long string. He fitted this string under his windbreaker and over the rolled up cloth. In order to have it stay in place, Ted put the string around his neck after he had made a loop under his armpit and over the wound. This was all over his jacket and when he went to tie this securely, he found he could not do it with one hand. Ted could not move his left hand enough to tie with it. So now what? Maybe he could hold one end with his teeth. It was difficult and required several tries but finally it was tied and seemed to have slowed the bleeding.

By now it was close to dark and Ted was far from home. Another big problem, is that whoever did the killing will want to eliminate any witness. If Ted went home now, they will follow him to his home and kill him, Ann, Jake and Lois. No, he definitely can't go home. Poor Ann will begin to worry about what happened when Ted doesn't come home. Eventually the cows will need to be milked, feeding done and other chores Ted normally takes care of. What will happen?

If Ted could find a place where there were lots of tracks maybe he could get his tracks lost in the shuffle, maybe go back to Millers old homestead. He will head there. All *at once, another shot rang out and a bullet hit a tree a few inches from Ted. Some bark was knocked off and hit his face. Immediately there was blood and his left eye had a cut above it on the eyebrow. That began to swell and his eye was partially closed. Bigger problems! Ted looked in the direction the shot seemed to come from. There was the guy he had wounded still coming after him. He was about one hundred twenty-five yards away. Ted really didn't want to kill anyone so he continued in a southwesterly direction, away from home. He felt very weak and faint and by now it was nearly dark.*

As Ted slowly walked, things began to fall in place. He had seen two large black cars go past his place at least twice in the last week. A guy at the hardware store said he thought there were some mobsters in town. He had seen these tough looking, well-dressed men as well as these big black cars. Very unusual for Spooner. We had all heard that Al Capone had property around here but many of us thought they were just rumors. Another thing, last week Ted took his .38-55 to Jim, a local gunsmith up by Springbrook, as it needed some work done on the action. They visited while he fixed it and Jim said, "A few days ago this big black Cadillac pulled up and two men got out. They were well dressed but rough looking. They wanted to know if I could fix guns. I told them it depends what is wrong with it. Anyway, one guy goes back to the car and brings out a Tommy Gun - Wow! He told me what was wrong and lucky for me I could fix it. One guy wanted to know if he could try it out and I said sure go ahead. He went out near the car, held the gun on his hip and fired off about ten rounds quicker than I could count. The guy dug out a $50 dollar bill and wondered if that would cover it. I had never seen a $50 dollar bill before but I said that would be fine. The men thanked him and got in the car and drove away." Ted bet these guys are the same ones that wanted the Tommy Gun fixed.

Afternoon of Labor Day, Monday, September 5, 1948

      Jim, Jed and I rode our bikes to Joe's place to see if he wanted to fish trout at the sand banks. His folks said he could go for a couple of hours. Joe took a fishing pole and all four of us rode out to Highway 53 and south to the Wild Life Road. We went east on this road, crossed the railroad tracks and continued on to the sand banks. No one else was there and we put worms on our lines, found a spot to fish from shore and started fishing. We all were near each other so we talked back and forth as we fished. Jim and Jed were telling Joe about Joe Pachoe and the tangle of trees he apparently spent most of the winter in a few years ago. Joe was really fascinated and wanted to see that place. I said that in order to really see the place we need a flashlight. Someday we will go. After about half-hour we decided to go to the big hole a little farther downstream. This was a really good looking large pool. We all put our baits in at the top of the pool and we planned to let each bait out to a different part of the pool. We were still letting out line when Joe said he had something on and it felt big. The rest of us pulled in our lines while Joe fought this fish. I could tell by the bend in his rod that Joe had a hold of a good sized fish. Joe played the fish and did a good job of it. We had no net so we told Joe to try to beach the fish on a sandbar toward the bottom of the pool.

      Finally, we saw the fish. It was a trout and a real beauty. Joe finally pulled the trout toward the sand bar and I was able to grab it by the jaw and lift it out. It was eighteen inches long and must have weighed three pounds. Joe wanted to keep it and he did. We put our lines out again but catching the big fish pretty much spoiled that pool for anymore good fishing.

      We pulled in our lines and headed for Joe's place, his big trout hanging on the handlebars of his bike. He was very proud. On the way we talked about the first football game which was going to be tomorrow. It sure seems that we all are pretty unsure and somewhat scared. Who are these kids we are going to play? Are they tougher, stronger, faster and more skilled than us? We finally agreed that they are freshmen just like we are and they are maybe asking the same questions about us.

We got to Joe's driveway and we stopped. Joe said he really enjoyed the morning and was looking forward to the game tomorrow even though he can't play yet. The three of us went to our homes. Both Jim and Jed were going on picnics with their families. Maybe we will too.

Tuesday, September 6, 1948

The first day of school and the first freshman football game. Jim, Jed and I walked to school. The buses arrive and mobs of kids get off, including Joe. This is the first time he ever rode a school bus, but it went OK. A couple of older kids ribbed him about being a new kid.

We went to our classes and there were a lot of new kids. Many were coming in from country schools that only went to eighth grade. Springbrook school goes through tenth grade but apparently this is the last year for ninth and tenth grade there. All of my classes looked good to me. The teachers were likeable and all the classes had from twenty-five to thirty-two students in them.

Our game was at 5:00 p.m. We already had our game jerseys and we got clean practice pants to wear for the game. We needed to transfer the knee pads and thigh pads from our dirty practice pants. Coach Jones told us to check the laces in our shoulder pads and replace any that looked worn out. Finally, we went out and warmed up. Barron freshmen were warming up also. Mom and Dad are both at the game.

The game started. We lost the coin toss and were on defense first. I started at left defensive back. Barron ran a T-formation similar to us. They had three large linemen and two large halfbacks that were also fast. We were able to keep them from getting a first down so they punted to us. I was our punt return man. I caught the ball and headed to my right, picked up a couple blocks and ran the ball to the Barron twenty-four yard line. Next play was a sweep to the right. Darrell carried and we had good blocks by 'Rough' and 'Tough' and we scored. I blocked the end and it felt good. The rest of the game went our way. Final score was Spooner 27 - Barron 0. I scored a touchdown on a dive play. That sure felt good.

Wednesday, September 7, 1948

The freshmen football team got lots of ribbing for beating up on Barron so badly. It was all good natured ribbing. There were lots of slaps on the back also. We travel to Ladysmith next Tuesday. Joe is able to practice and he will work out at inside linebacker and fullback. Practice was fun. There was a lot of hustle and we are pretty proud of the way we played against Barron. Ladysmith plays a double-winged T which means the halfbacks line up behind the end and their quarterback fakes the ball to the fullback and then he gives the ball to either halfback as they follow the blocks of the linemen. Some of the reserves run plays like we think Ladysmith will run. They play a 6-3 defense so the offense practices against that. Coach Jones puts in two new pass plays. One is a screen pass to either halfback. 'Rough' and 'Tough' really like screen passes. They really get downfield and knock people down.

In forestry class we are learning to identify all the tree species that grow around Spooner. We will also learn to identify samples of various species of boards. I wrote a letter to Savannah and told about my classes and our first football game. Dad is down to one ore train a week but he still works a lot of hours.

Friday, September 9, 1948

We have the last full contact practice before we play Ladysmith. Their offense is hard to stop with lots of traps. Our offense seems to really move the ball. One of our neighbor ladies works making wreaths at Hayward starting in October. She is talking to Mom about riding together and make wreaths. Mom and Dad have talked about it and Mom is tempted.

Mom has checked on bus and train schedules so I can visit Savannah during teachers convention. It looks like I would take the train to Bloomer and then take the bus to Antigo. There is an hour and half delay at Bloomer. Similar schedule on the return. There is a longer delay from bus to train. Tomorrow, Mom, Dad and I are going to take our boat and fish pan fish on Big McKenzie Lake.

Monday, September 12, 1948

I got a letter from Savannah. She told about her classes and she is very pleased with all of them. She did make the varsity band and was very pleased about that. Their freshmen football team also won.

We had a light practice as we ran through our plays and then our defense against their plays. We ran through all the special teams and worked on our new pass plays. The coaches handed out the white game jerseys that we will wear at Ladysmith as well as in school tomorrow. The bus will leave at 3:00 p.m. so we will miss part of seventh period class.

Tuesday, September 13, 1948

Ladysmith is a long trip, over an hour on the bus each way. Our defense did pretty good but gave up two touchdowns. Our offense really rolled - 37 points. Darrell scored twice on sweeps to my side. I scored twice on sweeps to his side. Fullbacks scored twice - once by Joe. 'Rough' and 'Tough' really can get downfield and knock the other guys down. We play Hayward next week.

Friday, September 16, 1948

We had a test in forestry about identifying tree species from their bark. I got a 100. Worked on the play where the quarterback rides the ball to the fullback while I flair out to the right. The quarterback looks right at the defensive end and finally pulls the ball out from the fullback and makes a move toward the end. When the end tries to tackle him he throws a pass to me. If the end lays back, the quarterback keeps the ball and runs off tackle with it. This play works very well in practice. Once I catch the ball, I am on my own.

On Saturday I am going to Joe's place. His dad is working up a field and has found some rocks that need to be picked. I expect that is an unpleasant job but it needs to be done.

Hayward plays a T-formation but uses a fair amount of 'man in motion' as part of their offense. They also have used some trick plays in the past so the coaches reviewed several trick plays that they may try to pull. The game is here at 5:00 p.m. on Tuesday. I wrote another letter to Savannah. Good night.

Tuesday, September 20, 1948

Spooner freshmen 27, Hayward freshmen 6. The offense really rolled. One touchdown from sweep right, one touchdown from sweep left. Joe scored a touchdown on a forty-one yard run right up the middle. We tried the play where the quarterback fakes to the fullback and then passes to me out on the flat. It worked great. I caught the ball and ran past the first defender. The safety came over and I switched the ball and stiff armed him and ran for a touchdown. We play at Cumberland next week.

Sounds like Mom is going to make wreaths. She says she will at least try it and hopes she can make a nice wreath and do it fast enough to keep up with the expected rate.

Oh, yes. This is freshmen initiation week at school. 'Rough', 'Tough', Joe and I bought our little green beanie. Cute!

Wednesday, September 21, 1948

There is a big change in plans. Three of the varsity halfbacks got hurt in Friday's game with Hayward. Coach Jones called Darrell and me into the office to talk to us. He said that the varsity coach and his assistant want Darrell and me to play with the varsity on Friday. They think we are the next best halfbacks on all of our football teams at Spooner. We would only be able to play in two quarters as no player in Wisconsin can play more than six quarters in a week. In the other two quarters, the junior varsity backs will do the best they can. They want the two of us to run the sweeps and catch the option pass after the fake to the fullback. They know this comes as a surprise to both of us but the coach said that they don't plan to ask us to carry the ball inside the ends. If that is alright with us, the varsity would like us to practice with them for about twenty to thirty minutes tonight and again tomorrow.

Darrell and I were completely surprised. We really didn't think we were anywhere near ready for varsity even though kids at smaller schools have to play varsity as freshmen. In fact, we met some kids from Shell Lake at the Hayward game and they said that three or four boys play for the Shell Lake varsity and one is a starter on the team. Both Darrell and I really wonder if we have enough experience to compete with these older, bigger, more experienced players from Cumberland. Coach Jones told us he will be coaching with the varsity Friday and he will only allow Darrell and me to participate on certain plays. He will watch over us if we agree to go to the varsity for this game only, unless the injured players are not able to play in the following game with Bloomer.

Darrell and I worked with our team until the varsity coach, Mr. Jensen called us over. He stopped practice and talked to the team and told them, "Three halfbacks were hurt against Hayward and most of you know that they can't play against Cumberland. I have asked a couple of junior varsity backs to practice with us as well as these two freshmen. They will only be asked to run the sweeps and catch passes. I do expect you older guys to accept them and help them.

They are a part of this team and I don't want any freshmen 'initiation' stuff going on with them. Understand?"

Cumberland plays a 5-4 defense and this was the first time Darrell and I had seen this. This meant the defensive end maybe crashed more rather than boxing. The cornerback behind him has outside responsibilities. This meant that I needed to decide if the end had outside or the cornerback did. I was to block whoever had outside responsibility.

We ran several sweeps with only moderate success. It seemed that the varsity guards were a little slower and didn't knock down defenders like the freshmen. The option passes worked great as the varsity quarterback was a very good athlete that could really run and he had a very quick release if he needed to pass. This play really puts pressure on the cornerback. Tackle the quarterback or cover me on the flat. Besides the back side end runs a deep route toward my side to draw the safety deeper and away.

No one gave us a hard time, but neither Darrell or I felt comfortable working with the varsity. Several of them did tell us that they really were happy that we were going to play with them. I guess they really needed us.

Darrell and I went back to our team. We were happy to see our team, however there seemed to be a strange feeling about our return. I sure hope we don't get caught not being a real part of either team. Darrell and I are both very much team players. This new attitude was hard to figure out. 'Rough', 'Tough' and Joe were all very happy to have us back. They also realized that we may only play two quarters against Cumberland. Maybe by then the varsity backs will be able to play and we can play the entire freshmen game, if needed.

We are supposed to decorate our beanies, carry upper-classmen's books, and bow down, too, if directed. Thursday evening all freshmen are to report to the high school gym for more initiation. We have heard stories of other initiations and we are very wary.

I wrote a quick letter to Savannah. Then had a good talk with Mom and Dad. They have concerns about safety with being asked to do a task that I may not be ready to perform. I could tell Mom was concerned. At the end of our discussion, Mom came and gave me a long hug. She held me at arms length and looked at me for several seconds and then gave me another hug. I can tell Mom is very concerned and I think she wanted to tell me more but we finally said goodnight.

Dad didn't say much. I think he approves but he was quiet. I went to my room and tried to write about what has happened. I am uncertain if I can help the varsity, missing the closeness of our freshmen team, initiation coming up and Mom and Dad's reaction seemed a little strange. I feel a little strange now, too. Good night.

Friday, September 23, 1948

The initiation went fine. In the end, all the freshmen threw their beanies into a small fire, if they wanted to. This was the end of the freshmen initiation.

We got our red game jerseys after practice on Thursday. My number was 56 and Darrell was 36. Cumberland is coming here and they have won two games and lost one at this point. Game time is 7:30 p.m. and we need to be to the locker room by 6:00 p.m. We are to be dressed by 6:45 p.m.

After the game - Spooner 27, Cumberland 6. Darrell and I didn't get into the game until Spooner's second possession. The quarterback called for sweep right which means Darrell carries and I block. The end crashed so I went for the cornerback as he tried to contain Darrell. Both guards pulled and took care of the end. The cornerback kept backing up so I blocked him out and Darrell cut inside of him. The right end helped on the tackle and then blocked the inside linebacker. The right guard continued up the hole in front of Darrell and flattened the safety. Darrell ran 62 yards for a touchdown. The crowd went wild and so did our team!

Just before halftime, the quarterback called the fullback option pass. He put the football in the fullbacks gut and went several steps toward the defensive end. The end went to tackle the fullback and the quarterback pulled the ball out and fired a pass to me. The cornerback came up to try to tackle me but I stiff armed him and went outside. Next came the safety and I could see our left end coming to help out. I switched arms and cut to my left which caused the safety to turn around just in time to get flattened by the end. I was in the open field and forty-two yards later - a touchdown.

Third quarter was my turn to sweep left. It worked like a charm. Darrell blocked his man out, both guards flattened their men and I scooted forty-eight yards for another touchdown. The place went wild. There were lots of back slaps. It felt like I was a part of the team. In the fourth quarter, the quarterback called the fullback option and kept the ball and ran for thirty-eight yards for a touchdown. Coach Jenson really had praise for our team.

Next is a non-conference game with Ashland. The game will be at Spooner. Ashland is a bigger school and their record is 4 wins and one loss. Our varsity record is also 4 wins and one loss to Ladysmith. This game will be on Friday night. Darrell and I may not have to play on the varsity, and we will find out early next week.

The Spooner freshmen will play the Ashland freshmen at Ashland at 5:00 p.m. next Tuesday. Apparently they have not lost a game yet either. Darrell and I hope we can play all four quarters with our guys. Ashland plays a 5-4 defense and are not big, but they are fast. Somehow Coach Jones found that information out from someone.

Saturday, September 24, 1948

This morning I rode my bike to Joe's place just south of Spooner. I found that a crew was there to fill the silo with corn silage. Joe told me that earlier his dad and a neighbor used a machine called a corn binder that cut the corn stalks and put them into a certain sized bundle. The bundle is tied with twine and dropped on the ground. A machine called a silo filler is set up by the silo and large pipes lead up to the top of the silo where a curved hood will direct the silage into the silo. The silo filler is run by a large flat belt that is run by a pulley on a tractor. The silo filler cuts the corn stalk into short lengths less than one inch long. There is a big blower as part of the machine that blows the silage up the pipe and into the silo.

Men with wagons begin to arrive and they go out into the cornfield and throw these corn bundles on the wagons. When the wagon is loaded, they head to the silo filler and pull up beside an apron that the bundles will be put on to be carried into the machine to be cut up.

Since the silage comes out and makes a pile in one spot in the silo, a distributor pipe is added to the hood. This has a long rope attached so it can be directed to all parts of the silo. Joe's job was to pull the rope to get the silage evenly distributed in the silo. He also was expected to pack the silage as he pulled the rope. This sounds like an easy job except - - - - the silage being blown into the silo falls everywhere, including on Joe and me because I helped Joe. In a few minutes we were covered with silage but it really did not get any worse.

The other thing Joe had to do was put a silo door in the proper opening as the silage got deeper and deeper. This only took a short time but Joe had to brace himself in the silo chute to put the door in place. It was about 30 inches wide and 30 inches tall. Finally, the silo filler was shut off and it was lunch time. Joe and I cleaned up the best we could and went to eat. There were eleven of us at the table and Joe's mom had made a wonderful meal which included roast beef and mashed potatoes.

During the meal, one of the men said he had heard that Spooner beat Cumberland in a football game and a couple freshmen halfbacks ran all over the place. "Who are these kids?" Joe's dad said, "One of them is sitting right beside you - meet Nick. And Joe is my son and he is a fullback and linebacker on the freshmen team with Nick."

This man had talked to his neighbor who had been

at the game and was really impressed. Spooner must have a good team. I told him that we play Ashland on Friday at Spooner and both teams have only lost one game. Darrell and I don't know if we need to play with the varsity because the injured halfbacks may be alright to play. We spent the rest of the day filling the silo but there was more silage than the silo could hold so we called a halt while a bundle of snow fence was hoisted up and set up on top because this silo has no roof. This made the silo about four feet higher. The last of the corn bundles were blown in and it just fit. One of the men said that the silage will settle and go down two to three feet in a few days. Anyway, the silo filler had its pipes removed and loaded on the apron. The belt was rolled up and stowed in the machine and the tractor hooked on and away it went to the next silo that needed filling. All of these men worked together to help each other and one neighbor owned the silo filler. Joe's mom says she likes her job at the bank.

Afternoon, Sunday, September 25, 1948

I helped Mom wash the windows on the outside of the house. Dad is driving a train today so I will try to write some more on my story, *The Mob and the Deer Hunter.*

What is Ted going to do about the guy trying to shoot him? Apparently he is following Ted's tracks and is intent on getting him. Ted came to a spruce swamp on his way to Millers' house. He was weak and felt faint but he immediately came up with a plan. There were several spruce trees that blew over a few years back. They would be tinder dry and would really burn. If he could get a fire started in those dead trees, maybe he could take his windbreaker and use sticks to prop it up like he was sitting by the fire.
Ted got busy the best he could in his weakened condition. He always carried a fire starting kit he made up that had wooden matches and birch bark in a small medicine bottle. He assembled small dry sticks under a place where

two spruce trees had fallen over each other. He found some sticks and took off his windbreaker after much pain. He propped the sticks in the wind breaker with his back to the direction he expected his pursuer to come from. He lit the tinder and it really took off burning. Ted moved to a spot about sixty feet from the fire and where he could watch his back trail. He stood behind a fairly large spruce with a low branch he could rest the .38-55 on and shoot if he had to.

By now it was nearly dark and Ted was getting colder as the temperature was down in the twenties. Ted watched the back trail and listened for any sounds. All at once, there he was! The light from the fire made this man visible to Ted.

Ted watched as the man moved to within about fifty feet of the propped up windbreaker. Ted had already cocked the hammer of the .38-55 and was sighting along the barrel, as looking through the sights would be useless as the light from the fire did not shine on the proper parts of the sights.

The man was unsteady as he moved but when he felt he was in his best position he raised his gun and fired! This was what Ted was waiting for. First, it was clear now that this man really meant to kill Ted. Second, the flash from the barrel of his gun would give Ted an opportunity to sight along the gun barrel, if only for an instant.

When the first shot rang out, there was a second shot a split second later. The pursuer fell to the ground and the propped up windbreaker fell over. Ted worked the action of the .38-55 and put another cartridge in the chamber. He watched the body of the man lying where it fell. There was no rolling around, no jerking of any kind. Ted watched for at least ten minutes and then went to his windbreaker and with great effort got it over his shoulders and loosely tied the arms in front of him. He took time to reload the .38-55. Its magazine held five rounds, plus one in the chamber. This meant that all of his ammunition was now in the gun.

Now it hit him. Ted had apparently killed another human being. He had no idea who it was. He did know this man somehow was connected with the killing he observed earlier. Apparently these men must be mobsters and must *have settled a score which Ted observed earlier. The man lying dead a few feet away must be one of the mobsters. Apparently failure to silence Ted might have meant the end to his story. The same as the guy killed earlier today.*

Ted had served in the military and had been trained to kill in many ways. Part of their training is to be able to accept killing another human being as part of their responsibility as a soldier in battle. If this had been in a war, Ted would have been able to accept the death of the enemy. Apparently the man lying a few feet away was the enemy but Ted had not been conditioned to that fact and now he felt a great guilt for ending this man's life. Apparently for the time being Ted was willing to forget that this man wounded him twice and had just tried to shoot him in the back as he sat by the fire. Ted finally began to get over killing the man but he still had misgivings about it. Now he wondered if other mobsters will pick up the trail and continue to come after him.

Ted had gotten warmed by the fire in the spruce swamp. He really worried about Ann and the kids. By now it was about 6:30 p.m. and Ann would have called the sheriff. He hoped they will respond quickly. He imagined they will follow his tracks using lanterns. There has not been any new snow today so they should be able to easily follow his tracks. Ted hoped Ann was able to get one of the neighbors to milk the cows and do whatever chores Ann could not do.

Ted knew he needed to get to the Miller house as there was a wood stove there and earlier today, Ted saw smoke coming from the chimney. The sky was clear and Ted could find the North Star and the Big Dipper. He reasoned that he had to head south-southwest to get to Millers house. He thought it must be a little less than a quarter of a mile. Ted felt weak but he started out. It didn't take very long before he bumped into a tree. It was dark, very, very dark.

Late Monday, September 26, 1948

Darrell and I split time with the freshman team and the varsity. Coach Jones told both of us that we will probably have to play against Ashland on Friday. Coach said, "We want both of you to play two quarters tomorrow." Coach Jones really feels bad for us and wished it didn't have to be like it is. He really seems sincere but both Darrell and I would rather just play with our freshmen buddies.

Mom and Dad have come to all the games and seem to really support me and enjoy the games. However, they both seem somewhat reserved, like something is bothering them. I hope no one is sick with something like cancer. They both appear healthy, but something in their demeanor doesn't seem right. I hope everything is OK.

Tuesday, September 27, 1948

Spooner freshmen 7, Ashland freshmen 0. This was by far the best team we played so far. Neither team could move the ball much and Darrell and I didn't play in the first half at all. In the fourth quarter their quarterback fumbled the football and we recovered it on the Ashland twenty-four yard line. Darrell swept to the right for eight yards to the sixteen yard line. Joe, the fullback, got three yards behind 'Roughs' block for a first down on the thirteen yard line. Next play was a sweep to the left and I carried for seven yards to the six yard line. Next play Joe got stopped for no gain. Third and three and we tried a pass to the right end in the end zone and it was deflected. Fourth and three and a time out was called. Coaches called for a fullback option pass. We looked at each other in the huddle after the play was called. Joe said, "Lets go do it." He reached out and put his hand on my shoulder before we broke the huddle. Our eyes met and I got the feeling that we were going to make this play work. The ball was snapped, quarterback rode the ball to Joe going off right tackle and the end tried to tackle Joe. The quarterback pulled the ball out, took two quick steps and faked the pass to me in the flat. I could see the defensive back coming up so I turned up field.

Just as the defender turned to see what the quarterback was doing, the defender made the choice to go for the quarterback, so he tossed a pass to me near the sideline. I caught the ball. By now the safety on that side tried to tackle me so I switched hands, cut left and stiff-armed the safety. Touchdown! Joe pounded behind 'Tough' and scored the extra point. This was a tough outfit we played but Coach Jones said, "We were tougher." Most of us had gotten banged up a little. Later, the Ashland coach came into our locker room and congratulated us on the victory and wanted to tell us that we were good sportsmen and several of his players thought we played hard but fair! That was certainly a nice gesture from the Ashland team. What we didn't know until later is that Coach Jones had gone to the Ashland locker room and praised their team for good, clean, hard hitting and good sportsmanship. No losers tonight. This team was definitely quick and faster than anyone we had played to date. Bloomer is next Tuesday for the freshmen football team.

When we got home from the game, we went in to the house and Mom and Dad told me that they had something to tell me. Please sit down. Oh, boy, here it comes.

I could tell that both Mom and Dad were under a great deal of duress and finally Mom said, "This is not how we wanted to tell you, but events have happened that leave us no option. You are adopted." The words hit like a ton of bricks. **You are adopted.** I was speechless. I could not believe it! Good thing I was sitting down because I would have fallen down. Mom and Dad both came to me and put their arms around me and hugged me - hard. I had many questions but finally Mom and Dad sat down and told me about the adoption.

Your birth mother was a young seventeen year old girl in a nearby town. You were born and this young girl felt she could not care for you properly so arrangements were made for us to adopt you. We were thrilled to be able to adopt you. You were a wonderful baby and we loved you from the time we brought you home.

Dad said, "The reason for telling you at this time is because your birth mother is very sick. Her husband contacted us with the request that she would like to meet her son before she dies. She is in the hospital at Hayward and time is very short. Perhaps we should go to her yet tonight, if it is alright with you."

My mind was reeling. This was very difficult for me to get straight in my mind. "The man that called with the request is your birth father. Sometime after you were born, your mom and dad married and you have a twelve-year-old brother and a ten-year-old sister. The family lives near Hayward," Mom said. I have a brother and a sister? And another Dad? All this new information was difficult to understand.

Mom said, "You will always be our son. We love you and always will. For as long as your dad and I are alive we will love you like a son. If you would like to get to know your new found family and want to share your life with them, we will understand. But we want you to be our son, forever."

I asked, "What is wrong with my birth mom?" Mom said, "I don't know except there is not much time, a few days maybe. Perhaps we should go to the hospital tonight and try to see her."

We got in the car and headed to Hayward. On the way Mom told me that my birth mothers name is Jean and she is 32 years old. Her husband is Howard, the twelve-year-old boy is Sam and the ten-year-old girl is Carol.

We arrived at the hospital and were told that we could visit Jean and they gave us the room number. We approached the room and I was very nervous. Mom went in first and introduced herself to Jean and the rest of the family. Dad and I came in a little later and I walked up to the bed. Here was a very pretty lady, medium long hair with a big smile. She held up her hands toward me and beckoned me to come to her. She said my name and clasped my hands in her hands. She looked into my eyes and I looked into hers. This was an exciting moment. This was a path I had not traveled on before, or ever thought I would travel.

Dad introduced himself to Jean and her husband Howard. I looked at the kids and saw me when I was twelve years old. I could not believe it. Sam was a carbon copy of me! Ten-year-old Carol had many similar features to me. Howard looked a little like me also. All seemed friendly and happy that we came.

Jean told us, "The doctors told me the I have only a few days left and I wanted to see my first born son. I went to the County Judge and explained that I wanted to find you and he gave permission for me to meet with the proper people to begin searching for you. This took some time and in the meantime I thought back to those sad days over 15 years ago. I still had a year of high school. I had no job and my dad had died the year before so Mom was the sole support for me and two brothers and sisters. Howard was in the Army and still had one and one-half years left to serve. Believe me, the decision to give you up was very painful and I could not even see you after you were born. I cried for several days but I was assured that you went to a wonderful home where you would be loved and well cared for. I can see you have grown into a handsome, young man and I can tell your mom and dad really love you. I bet you are a good student and have many friends."

Jean wanted me to tell her about me so I mentioned school, the football team and camping on Beaver Brook this past summer. I told her about Savannah and a few other things. Then I asked her if she had a career besides raising Sam and Carol. Jean said, "I took classes to become a nurses aid and did that for several years. I took classes to become a nurse and recently became a nurse at this hospital. I wish I could have continued being a nurse but it was not to be."

Mom said, "It was wonderful that you could see Nick after all these years. We are happy to have Nick meet you and the rest of the family. I think we better let you get some rest now."

The ride back to Spooner was quiet. Apparently we were all deep in our own thoughts. I know I was. I was proud of Mom and Dad honoring this dying woman's request to see her son she gave up so many years ago. That was not an easy decision because now they would have to tell me that I was adopted. I wonder when my folks were going to tell me - if ever. Actually I would have gotten along just fine my entire life without knowing I was adopted. The only thing that rears its head is there some medical problems that I have inherited that I should know about? What is Jean dying from? Is it something I have inherited?

Mom and Dad have certainly given me a wonderful home, lots of love and have been wonderful parents. They may feel that I think less of them now. Actually, I think more of them for doing all they did for me and then are willing to share me with my birth mom, not knowing what might come from it. Having a brother and sister is real hard to get used to. Will we ever spend time together? It isn't like a divorce where the parents share the children. Only time will tell.

Boy, this day got long and had very wide emotional swings. Good night.

Friday, September 30, 1948

I have had a hard time concentrating on school work and football since Tuesdays bombshell. Apparently Jean is still hanging on. Mom stays in contact with Howard. It seems as if I have two worlds now. Darrell and I have to suit up for the varsity game at Ashland. All the injured varsity backs are ready to play but Coach Jensen wanted us to be ready in case we were needed.

We kicked off to Ashland and they ran it back for a touchdown. Our turn and we moved the ball but could not score. The score at halftime, Ashland 7, Spooner 0. Second half we got to fourth and three for a touchdown and could not get it in. Finally, late in the game behind by seven, Coach Jensen put Darrell and me in the game. He told us to tell the quarterback to run sweep right first then come back

52

with sweep left. The sweep right starts and the defensive end on my side crashes and I block him into the line. The cornerback has outside contained and the guards both pull and take the cornerback down and continue on and take out the safety. Darrell scoots around all of these blocks and runs to the 17 yard line before the other safety runs him out of bounds.

Next play is sweep left and I carry the ball. Our blockers get their men and I am going down the sideline when the other safety tried to tackle me. I switched the ball to my right arm, cut right and stiff-armed with my left arm. I got tackled right at the goal line but it was a touchdown. The extra point was a fake to the fullback and a short pass to the right end and it worked. Ashland 7, Spooner 7 and that is the way the game ended. I wrote a short letter to Savannah. I will go to Antigo in one week. Small game hunting season starts tomorrow. 'Rough', 'Tough', Joe and I are going to try for squirrels, partridge and rabbits across the railroad tracks from Joe's house.

Saturday, October 1, 1948

During the night I thought about my birth mother. This entire happening has my head spinning. I decided that I should try to get to know her better before it is too late. Dad is working today but I will ask Mom to take me to see her.

Mom is able to drive me to Hayward and is happy to do it. So I call 'Tough' and told him I could not go hunting today. On the way to Hayward, Mom told me that she and Dad did not want to push me at all and hoped I would want to spend time with her. We were able to see Jean and she was by herself. She was very happy to see us and wanted me to give her a hug, which I did. She wanted me to pull a chair up close so I could hold her hand as we talked. She told me about her family and how she and Howard met. At the time I was born her life was in turmoil. She was young and was not prepared or ready to raise me. Howard was in the army and would be for another year and one half. She said, "Giving

53

you up was by far the hardest thing I had ever had to do. My heart aches just thinking of you. When I knew my time was short, I knew I had to try to find you, to see how you turned out and to let you know that I love you and I always will. I also know your mom and dad love you and are wonderful parents. Ever since I gave you up there was a part of me that was missing, but now I am whole again. I feel redemption for not being able to have you with me and being able to care for you as you grew up." She continued, "Not a day went by that I didn't wonder where you were, what you were doing, and if were you healthy? What did you look like? I hoped you were a good boy, not trouble at school or with law enforcement."

"Seeing you and hearing you tell me things you have done, tells me that my most selfish wishes have come true. You are a wonderful young man that anyone would be very proud to call their son. Seeing you now makes me so proud. I don't want to leave, but I know I must. The emptiness in my heart is now full because I have been able to see you and have you by my side."

I felt my eyes were beginning to tear up so I left the room for a few minutes. Mom and Jean visited. I felt very sad for Jean. She seemed like such a nice person but her days are getting short. It just does not seem right. What about Sam and Carol? They will not have a mother. That must be very hard for them. It will be hard for me even though I just met Jean a few days ago. This entire happening is confusing and hard for me to be comfortable with.

I went back to Jean and sat by the bed. I could sense that she was tired so we just looked at each other and smiled. I sat there for at least thirty minutes and finally Jean fell asleep. During that time, I felt a very strong attraction to Jean. Maybe this was some hidden force reserved for a child and its birth mother. This force seemed to fill me up and make me feel warm. I wonder if Jean was feeling this force also. It made me want to stay by her. Finally, a nurse came in and asked us to leave as Jean needed to rest. I asked the nurse for a couple of minutes and went and asked Mom if she would mind if I gave Jean a kiss. Mom held me and told me, "You go kiss your mother." I walked up and kissed Jean on the forehead. By now I had to leave. Mom put her arm around me and we left Jeans' room. Halfway down the hall we stopped and I cried on Mom's shoulder. She cried with me. Finally we reached the car and went home. I am one confused boy.

Late Saturday, October 1, 1948

Mom and I got home by early afternoon and Dad had just got off the road. He asked me if I wanted to go partridge hunting and I said, "Sure." We got our shotguns and shells, put on hunting jackets and headed to several logging roads Dad knew about.

I had a beautiful side by side, 20 gauge double-barreled shotgun that Grandpa Joe gave me last year. It has two triggers and the right barrel is open choked and the left barrel is full choked. This means the left barrel has a shot pattern that does not spread as much as the open choke barrel. The gun is a Fox Model B and I have high brass number 6-shot in the left barrel and low brass number 6-shot in the right barrel.

Dad told me how to shoot partridge by pointing at them and not really aiming. He told me to practice by looking at a target and then rapidly bringing my gun up and pointing it at the target. Now look and sight down the gun to see how accurately you pointed. I do this in the winter, in my room or any place. I do this many times a day all winter and I can get pretty good at pointing at where I am looking. I was anxious to try this on flying partridges.

On the way to our hunting spot, Dad asked how my visit with Jean went. I could not answer for at least a minute. Finally I told my dad, "I am really confused. Just a few days ago I found out I was adopted and that was very difficult to comprehend. Then I found out my birth mother, Jean, is dying and wants to see me. Jean seems really nice and I am very sad that she will die soon. I found out I have a brother, Sam, and a sister, Carol. They seem very nice and Sam and I look a lot alike. On the way home from seeing Jean, Mom pointed out that now I may have new aunts and uncles, cousins, grandmothers and grandfathers. I also have a new father, Howard. I don't think I am ready to find out about these new relatives at this point. You and Mom have been my parents and we all love each other and we are a happy family. I don't want that to change."

Dad said, "It doesn't have to change. Jean does not want to try to get you back. She made that very clear. She just wanted to see you before she dies. Your mom and I think that our lives, meaning all three of us, can continue pretty much as it was before. At least we certainly hope it can."

"Some issues that need to be understood are: Do you have some genetic traits that put you at risk for certain diseases? In other words, do Jean and Howard have tendencies toward certain diseases that you may have inherited. The other issue is that in most states, including Wisconsin, first cousins cannot legally marry. Since Jean and Howard live at Hayward, maybe other brothers and sisters live nearby, in fact there may be some of your new first cousins going to school with you. Pretty scary, huh? Your mom and I will find out who your new found relatives are so you will not unknowingly want to marry one of your first cousins."

We arrived at our hunting spot. I was not exactly in the mood to hunt partridge but off we went. The logging roads are quite often temporary trails used to get the logs out of a particular part of the woods. They may remain open for several years and sometimes they are used again in a few years. For whatever reason, white clover tends to grow wherever the soil in a woods is disturbed. Partridge, or ruffed grouse, love clover leaves and they seem to end up on these trails eating clover leaves at the end of the day. Partridge hunters know this so they do what Dad and I are doing - slowly walking, side by side, on these trails hoping to flush a 'thunder bird' that we can get a shot at. Dad has already told me 'no ground swatting'. In other words, I can only shoot at a partridge that is flying. We are hoping that there are large numbers of partridge as winter conditions were good and so was spring weather, so hopefully mother partridge raised large broods of ten to fifteen chicks.

After about ten minutes of walking, a grouse flushes on Dad's side of the road. He takes a shot with his 12-gauge Remington Pump gun and misses. A few steps farther and I get a chance to try my pointing method of shooting partridge. I shoot and I see lots of feathers fly. I reload and go look for the bird. I found it, admired it and put it in the game pouch of my hunting coat. A few minutes later Dad scores a hit. Even though there are a lot of leaves we were able to see most of the birds we flushed. I ended up with three birds and Dad had four. I had only one miss so I was happy. It was getting hard to see by the time we got back to the car. We both agreed it was a beautiful fall afternoon and we had a great time. We unloaded our guns and put them in cases and headed for High Street.

Monday, October 3, 1948

The freshmen play at Bloomer on Tuesday. Darrell and I practice with both the freshmen and varsity. Darrell and I both feel we are not as much a part of our freshmen team as we would like and really feel like we don't fit in with the varsity, even though they try to make us feel welcome. It comes down to the fact that lowly freshmen simply do not have the same social standing as the juniors and seniors on the football team. Even the two sophomores on the varsity feel about the same as Darrell and I do. Bloomer is defending champs from last year and they have only lost one game. The freshmen team has not lost yet so our teams will have their hands full. Tonight we worked on our screen passes to the halfback and draw plays. Darrell and I were the main halfbacks that ran these plays. Apparently Bloomer has a very good defensive line and really comes hard on pass plays. We will see.

Yesterday I helped Dad paint the south side of our house. In the afternoon, I just laid around and listened to

the Green Bay Packers playing the Detroit Lions.   Tobin
Rote is the Packer quarterback and Don Hutson and Billy
Thornton are the receivers. The Packers won 27 to 24. I had
a hard time concentrating on anything except trying to digest
the news about Jean. I felt a great sadness when I thought
about her. Death is still very hard for me to understand. I
know it is final for earthly things. I still don't understand a
persons soul. Does a persons soul really exist? When I die
will my soul meet souls of other people that have died? Will
my soul go to heaven or am I not a good enough person to
have my soul go there? Maybe I won't go there but maybe
go to Hades.

I wonder how Jean is today. I wonder what is wrong
with her. Is it something that will make me sick and die at a
young age? Perhaps Mom will find out what is wrong with
her. All of this seems like a big load for a fifteen-year-old
boy. I will take it a day at a time and hope for the best.

Tuesday, October 4, 1948

Spooner freshmen 7, Bloomer freshmen 6. It was
a very tough game. Darrell and I played the first half and
Darrell had a long run on a sweep right that took the ball
down to the Bloomer nine yard line. We ran the fake to the
fullback and the quarterback hit me with a pass and I got to
the two yard line. Two runs over 'Rough' and 'Tough' and
Joe was in the end zone. We kicked the extra point. We
kicked off after the touchdown and Bloomer ran it back for
a touchdown. Bloomer lined up to try a run for the extra
point. They ran a sweep toward me at left defensive back.
Earlier in the game they tried this play and I waited to see
what would develop and they gained eighteen yards before
we stopped them. I decided that I would come up hard and
at least take out the main interference which I did and got a
hand on the runners foot. This was enough to slow the play
and Joe came from his linebackers position and stopped their
halfback for no gain. That was all the scoring and our team
is still undefeated.

We play the Rice Lake freshmen next Tuesday at

Spooner. Friday morning I will get on the train at Spooner and get off at Bloomer. After a delay, I get on a bus and take it to Antigo to see Savannah. I really need to see her. I hope she can help me understand all the recent events in my life. I am really looking forward to spending two days with Savannah and her friends and family.

Thursday, October 6, 1948

Spooner varsity 21, Bloomer varsity 14. It was a very tough game. Bloomer had a bunch of hard hitting, big players. We couldn't do much with them with our regular plays. They seemed to have us scouted and we just could not get going. Our new plays worked great. A screen pass to Darrell went for fifty-two yards and a touchdown. I ran a draw play for sixty-one yards and a touchdown. We faked the screen to Darrell and ran a quarterback draw for thirty-one yards and a touchdown. Bloomer had the best defensive line we had seen in the conference. But their aggressiveness played into our hands. We are 4 - 1 in the conference. Bloomer is also 4 - 1, Rice Lake is 5 - 0. We play Rice Lake on Friday, October 14th at Spooner. If we can beat them we can share the conference title.

Mom went to see Jean today and she was very weak. Her sister, Joan, was at the hospital and Mom had a nice visit with her. She told Mom she would find out if there was any underlying genetic problems with Jean or Howard. She also would make a list of all the grandparents, aunts, uncles and first cousins and their ages. She would also list their addresses. Mom found out that Jean was dying from leukemia.

Friday, October 7, 1948

I am getting on the train at 7:45 a.m. Mom packed a small suitcase for me. Mom and Dad were both at the depot to see me off. Mom gave me a big, long hug and Dad gave me a firm handshake. They told me to say hello to Savannah and her parents and to have a good time. Between the train ride and the bus ride I will have a least six hours of riding or waiting. I will write some more on my possible book, *The Mob and the Deer Hunter.*

Ted stumbled and bumped into trees he could not see. He was moving and hopefully in the right direction. Eventually Ted could make out things by the very faint star light. He missed the Miller house but, all at once, he could smell wood smoke. He turned and followed the smell of smoke and, in a few minutes, he could make out the house. He found the door and went in and it was warmer in the house. He knew where the woodstove was so he went to it and he could see a faint glow around the door. He opened the door and enough light came out to see there was a small pile of firewood a short distance from the stove. He carefully put three sticks of firewood in the stove and blew on the coals to ignite the wood. In a few minutes the wood started to burn so he closed the stove door. Now he could not see well because he had been looking into the bright light of the fire. In a few minutes he could see pretty good again.

Ted knew he should expect some mobsters to come after him. They will follow his tracks using a lantern or flashlight. Ted needed to find a window where he could look in the direction that he had come from to get to the house. He also reasoned that he needed to get out of the house if he saw lantern lights approaching. He was concerned that they maybe would have a Tommy Gun. If they did, they may blast the house thinking he was in it. He went outside to the right of where his tracks were leading to the house. He sought a clump of trees that he could hide in but also a lower branch he could rest his .38-55 in order to shoot, if needed. He still felt weak and his eyebrow was so swelled up that he could only see a little out of his left eye.

Ted used the back door and he did find a clump of three white oaks in the proper place. There was no branch to rest his gun on, so he started feeling around with his foot and he found a branch with a fork on it which was too long but if he slanted it enough, the fork would be at the correct

60

height. He went back into the warmer house to wait for the mobsters or the sheriff.

Ted knew there were a couple of old wooden chairs in the house the last time he was there. He stumbled around and found one which he took over near a window that provided a view of his approach to the house. By now about one and one-half hours had passed since he left the burning fallen tree at the spruce swamp. He was very weak and sleepy and it felt like blood was running down his back from the wound on his left shoulder. He thought about Ann and the kids. Certainly they would be very concerned, wondering what had happened to Ted.

Finally, he could see a light in the distance. It was going at right angles to the house and was getting fainter. Ted wondered what it was and then it hit him. Whoever it is, is following his tracks and he went past the house until he smelled the smoke. He now realized that before long the light would be coming toward the house. In a few minutes, here came not one light but two.

Ted went out the backdoor and found his clump of white oaks. They were about sixteen inches in diameter and would provide some protection from gunfire if it occurred. The lights came closer and stopped about fifty feet from the house. Ted's clump of trees was about seventy feet from the men. He could hear them saying something between themselves and, all at once, one man opened up with the Tommy Gun and fired about fifty rounds into the house. He apparently reloaded and the two of them went in the front door. In a few minutes another short burst of shots occurred.

The men came out of the house and went to the small barn. The man with the Tommy Gun fired about fifteen or twenty rounds into the barn. The two men went back into the house and in a few minutes opened the back door and examined the tracks Ted made in the snow. By this time, Ted had gotten into position to be able to fire his .38-55 toward the back door. The two men pointed at the tracks Ted made and slowly followed them about twenty feet when the man with the Tommy Gun saw Ted in the clump of trees. He held the Tommy Gun at his hip and opened up. This is what Ted was waiting for, the light from the gun being fired and he could sight along his own gun and start shooting. Ted fired even as the bullets from the Tommy Gun were hitting around him. Ted's aim was true and he hit the man with the Tommy Gun and he fell, apparently very badly wounded. The other man had a handgun and was shooting wildly. His gun ran out of ammo and he ran over and grabbed the Tommy Gun and ran back behind the house. In a few minutes, Ted could see this man leaving the area, following their tracks away from the house. The other man that Ted shot lay still. The man had dropped his lantern and it landed upright and was still working. Ted watched the man for at least ten minutes and then cautiously approached him. Now he could see because of the lantern light. The man was dead. Ted's shot had hit him in the chest.

Who was this man? He appeared to be about fifty years old, heavy build, but less than six feet tall. Apparently there must be great need to get rid of Ted as a long distance witness to a murder. There is no way Ted could identify any of the three people involved in the murder Ted saw happen earlier in the day. This man may have been one of those shooters. He certainly is cold blooded enough as he was certainly trying to kill Ted.

Ted wondered what he should do. The other mobster apparently left, following his tracks the way he and the dead man made on the way in. Ted now had a lantern and he also could follow the tracks back home. A couple of reasons against that are first, to follow the tracks Ted made all day would be at least three miles. Ted did not think he had the energy to walk that far and secondly, Ted fully expected the sheriff to be following those tracks right now and they could help him get home or to a doctor.

While Ted was contemplating what to do he heard several gunshots a great distance away. It sounded like the Tommy Gun which has a low pitched staccato sound. There were also several shots, not from the Tommy Gun. Ted certainly wondered what all the shooting was about. There *has been entirely too much shooting in these dark Wisconsin woods lately. Ted decided to stay in the house. Actually, he really didn't have an option. He had gotten progressively weaker and now was feeling very faint.*

October 7, 1948

I am on the bus going to Antigo, Wisconsin. I switched from the train to a bus at Bloomer, Wisconsin. The bus will follow Highway 64 to Antigo which is about 150 miles from Spooner. Highway 64 goes through several small towns but Medford and Merrill are fairly large. The bus rolls into Antigo about 2:00 p.m. and there is Savannah and her mom to meet me. Savannah gave me a big hug and we climbed into Casey's car and Kathy dropped us off at the Antigo High School. That school is way bigger than Spooner High School. Savannah wanted us to go to a pep fest for the big game tonight. Rhinelander is Antigo's biggest rival and this is a real big game.

Savannah lead me into the high school gym which was crammed with students and adults. This gym is bigger than Spooner's and it was rocking. The pep band was really sounding great. The Antigo Red Robins football team came on the floor and the place went wild. Cheerleaders turned cartwheels, some waved flags as they led the team out. Also present were several bells of all sizes and they were ringing.

Finally the two team captains came out carrying the bell since Antigo won the game last year. The bell used to be on a paddlewheel boat that ran on the Wisconsin River in Rhinelander, about forty-five miles north of Antigo. Apparently this paddlewheel boat burned and the bell was salvaged by a man named Shepard. He may have owned the boat.

Anyway, Antigo and Rhinelander were bitter rivals then so he proposed 'The Battle For The Bell' beginning just after the turn of the century. The bell was mounted on a large backboard of beautiful wood. The score of each game is engraved on plaques and mounted on the wood. Savannah thought that the series was about even.

The head football coach came out and spoke to the crowd. He told about three Rhinelander players that were very good. One was a linebacker, another was the quarterback and the third was the fullback. He said Antigo will need to really play well as a team because Rhinelander is a very good team.

Next, the rest of the football coaches were introduced and two of them spoke briefly. The team members names were read off and each player went up and rang the bell as his name was read. The players wore their red game jerseys and each player was loudly recognized by whistles, shouts, clapping and bell ringing. Since there were over fifty players, this took some time and a great deal of energy was expended. Savannah cheered and clapped loudly.

Finally, the high school principal came out and addressed all those in the gym. He also praised the football team and sent a strong message about good sportsmanship. He encouraged the students to cheer, ring bells and enjoy this exciting football game, but most of all be good sportsmen, win, lose or tie. This exciting event was finished and people were leaving the gym.

Savannah had made plans to meet her three friends in the gym lobby. All three came out of the crowd and Savannah introduced me to Sandy, Cathy and Ann. All three seemed a little shy but all were good looking, neat girls. Cathy was about as tall as Savannah, Sandy and Ann were a little shorter but all were slim and all easily smiled. About then Savannah's dad Elon came out of the gym and came over to greet me. He seemed very happy to see me. I am pretty sure he made all the noise in the old house at the lake.

Savannah took me to her locker and picked up books and things. This school is big, way bigger than Spooner, but her locker was about the same as mine. We met the other girls and started for Savannah's house. These girls were really excited about the upcoming football game. There was non-stop talking on the way home. They all made me feel welcome but all four could really talk.

We got to Savannah's house which is about eight

blocks from school. Elon arrived from school and they were interested in how I was doing with my football playing. Elon felt sorry for me for having to play on the varsity as a freshman. I told about doing my 'Crazy Legs' Hirsch moves in the woods this summer. I told them that I really felt my ball shifting and stiff arm have been a big help on several long runs.

Elon had to be to the football stadium by 5:30 p.m. as he has to help with crowd control. He had already talked to Savannah about loading all four girls, me and Kathy into the car and getting us to the stadium which was about one and one-half miles from their home. Kathy had supper ready and we ate. At 5:15 p.m. the girls showed up and we all got stuffed into Elon's car and headed to the stadium.

The game starts at 7:30 p.m. but by 5:30 p.m. there were already several dozen people in the stadium. Savannah and her friends were going to stand on the east end of the football field. We bought our tickets and headed to a spot by the ropes on the east end. Cathy and Ann were planning to meet their boy friends at the game. Both play on the Antigo freshmen team so I was looking forward to meeting them. Sandy was hoping a boy in her civics class would be there, but she really did not have a boy friend.

Arriving two hours before the game starts sounds crazy but I could see why. Mobs of people kept coming as did the bells. All sizes of bells. A few large bells on trailers came in, smaller ones carried on carts and wagons. There were cow bells and sleigh bells. There were hundreds of bells and the place was crammed with people.

Finally, the teams came out to warm up. Antigo stayed on the west end and Rhinelander came to our end. Rhinelander had green and white colors and Antigo had cardinal jerseys with white pants. Both teams had a lot of big players, mostly seniors and juniors. About this time the boyfriends of Cathy and Ann joined our little group. Al was Cathy's friend and played halfback on his team. Pat was Ann's friend and played guard. Pat was sporting a black eye and both boys were about my size and seemed like friendly guys and we could easily talk. About this time, the boy from Sandy's class showed up and joined our group. His name was Ron.

I noticed the name for the Rhinelander team is 'The Hodags'. I asked Savannah what a Hodag was. She told me that about the turn of the century a mysterious animal was trapped in a cave west of Rhinelander. It had big bog eyes, big spines on its back and tail. It had huge long claws and big sharp teeth. Apparently it ate white bulldogs. The same man that got the 'Battle for the Bell' started made the discovery. He contacted the Smithsonian in Washington, D. C. and told them about this newly discovered animal called the Hodag. They apparently sent representatives to view this strange animal but by the time they arrived, the animal had escaped. However, the legend of the Hodag was begun. The man, Shepard, was a notorious prankster and the Hodag was his greatest prank.

The game started and so did the bells. Hundreds of bells ringing most of the time. These two teams played hard hitting, rough football. Antigo had two good runners and scored first. Rhinelander came back on a long run and the score was tied and that is the way the first half ended.

Rhinelander took the second half kickoff and ran it back for a touchdown and the lead. Antigo got its runners going and tied the score early in the fourth quarter. Antigo recovered a fumble on the Rhinelander twenty-nine yard line. They moved the ball to the six yard line and had third down. Antigo faked a run around the right end and the quarterback kept the ball and looked like he would score as this play was right in front of our group. The Hodag linebacker the coach had talked about tackled the quarterback on the one yard line. Now it was fourth down and one yard to go. Score was tied with less than one minute to play. Antigo took a time out. The crowd was going crazy and so were the bells. Al and Pat said that Antigo had a decent field goal kicker and this week they practiced often. Time out was over and Antigo came out and lined up to kick a field goal. Rhinelander took a time out. More tension, more bell ringing. The time out was over and teams lined up again. Antigo was going to try a field goal. The ball was snapped - it's a fake! The holder takes the ball and throws a pass to the right end who was not covered and Antigo is in the lead. Wow!

Antigo has to kick off and they remember that Rhinelander ran it back for a touchdown. It is a squib kick that bounces to about the middle of the Rhinelander team and there is no run back. There is time for one play and a long pass is tried. The pass is incomplete and time runs out. Antigo wins and the team picks up the board with the bell on it and runs out on the field with it.

The bells are beginning to ring less as the crowd begins to leave. This was quite the football game. Savannah and her friends were to meet Elon after the game and they would be dropped off at a restaurant near home. The three boys would meet the group at the restaurant. The girls all lived nearby so they could walk home later in the evening. We had a great time at the restaurant. There was lots of music, lots of kids and we all had hamburgers and malts. Finally, everyone went home as it was after midnight.

The next morning, Kathy had breakfast ready and we ate. Discussion about the game was the main topic. After eating, I had made up my mind to tell Savannah and her parents that I was adopted and maybe they can help me understand my feelings. When I told them, there was a look of disbelief but it did not last long because Savannah said she was adopted too. Wow! I told about Jean being very sick and may die soon and I had very mixed and strange feelings toward her. She is my birth mother and I feel a very strong attachment to her even though I have only known her for a few days.

Savannah said she doesn't know who her birth mother is but Elon and Kathy told her she was adopted when she was about four years old. She wonders who her mother is, who her father is, where they live and if there are other brothers and sisters, aunts, uncles, and grandparents. Savannah said she is comfortable knowing she is adopted but she does think about her birth mother sometimes. She reached out and held my hand and said, "I know what you are going through now. With Jean so very sick, it is sad that you just found out about her, and met her recently, and now she is about to die."

Kathy said they don't know anything about Savannah's birth mother. They have also wondered about any genetic tendencies and who Savannah's relatives are. It was very kind of your mom and dad to honor Jean's request to see you before she died. I am sure that your wonderful mom and dad spent much time agonizing whether to allow Jean to see you. They very likely realized the turmoil your life would become by hearing the news that you were adopted. Your mom and dad must have felt the love between the three of you was so strong that even this tremendous shock would not harm the wonderful relationship you share with them. Elon agreed with Kathy and told me that the love he saw between my parents and me is so strong that you all will be able to get through this. Finding out you now have a younger brother and sister and another Dad will take some time to sort out and maybe you and your siblings will become good friends and spend time together. Maybe your mom and dad will be happy to have your brother and sister spend time with you at your home. Maybe you will spend time with them at your new dad's home. No matter how things go in the future, remember, your mom and dad love you and have been wonderful parents and always will love you.

I really felt much better after our talk over the breakfast table. I like Kathy and Elon about the same way I love Mom and Dad. They are very nice, caring people. Elon wanted to take Savannah and me to a beautiful spot on the Wolf River. He has fished there but has never taken Savannah there.

We drove about twenty miles north and got on Langlade County Highway A and took it to the Wolf River. This is a very famous white water river in east central Wisconsin. The river drops rapidly in the area of the Highway A bridge. Elon took us down stream along the west bank of the Wolf. There are lots of large boulders in the river and the water is really moving fast. After about a quarter mile, Elon stopped and pointed out an inside curve where the river turns toward the east-southeast. Elon said he has caught many nice trout out of that hole. The biggest was about three pounds. The water is so fast and turbulent that you must use a Wolf River rig to fish in this river. All it is, is a staff with a pointed end that, when you are in the river, you push the staff firmly into the bottom of the river. Next, you carefully move your downstream foot in front of the staff. Bring your other foot even with the other and then pull up the staff and relocate it to move again. Also, fishermen that wear chest waders need to put a belt around their waist outside of the waders because, if you fall down and you don't have a belt on, your waders can fill with water and keep pushing you down stream. You would not be able to regain your footing. People have died in this river by getting knocked down and being unable to stand up.

The Wolf River is a beautiful fast moving river - far different from Beaver Brook back home. Savannah and I were very impressed with this wild river and maybe someday we may bring our spinning gear and Mepps spinners and challenge this exciting river.

Savannah and I spent the afternoon talking about school and a lot of other things. The attraction between us is very strong. We both felt the urge to hold each other like we did in my tent on Beaver Brook last summer. We held hands and looked at each other. My attraction to Savannah has not diminished but my respect for her is at a very high level and I plan to admire Savannah from afar. We both feel that in time we will be mature enough to address our attractions in an appropriate manner.

The weather was spectacular and it was a warm October afternoon and evening. Kathy and Elon organized a cookout by late afternoon. Savannah asked her friends to come if they could on such a short notice. Maybe Savannah had forewarned the girls because all three were able to come. Kathy cooked bratwurst over the outdoor fireplace. These little sausages in a bun were really tasty. These were new to me and Elon said they came from Sheboygan, Wisconsin.

By the time it got dark, Savannah turned some music on, outside lights came on and there was a party atmosphere. Also about this time, Al and Pat showed up. These are the boyfriends of Cathy and Ann. Not long afterward, Ron came walking into the light. He is Sandy's friend that met her at the game last night.

The small party was great. Just visiting, drinking soda and later Kathy brought out some sloppy joes and brownies. Eventually the party broke up and everyone left. It took two hours to write the happenings of today. Good Night.

Early Sunday, October 9, 1948

The bus to Bloomer would leave Antigo at 8:30 a.m. Kathy had breakfast ready at 7:30 and Elon and Savannah took me to the bus. I had thanked Kathy for a wonderful stay and did the same for Elon and Savannah. The bus arrived and Savannah took me in her arms, looked me in the eye and said, "Stay strong, strong, strong. The near future will be challenging, but you are up to it. I love you." She pulled me to her and gave me a kiss. I got on the bus and decided to write some more on my story, *The Mob and the Deer Hunter.*

Ted waited in the old Miller house. At least an hour passed and no one came. He could feel more and more blood flowing out of his shoulder wound. He realized that his time was running out and he needed to get home and then to a doctor. He checked the lantern and saw there was enough kerosene to last for more than an hour. He pulled out his compass and realized that he could read the compass and follow a path toward his house. He also realized that if he went northwest from the Miller house, he could reach his home in about one-half mile. He wondered if he could get home without collapsing.

Ted checked the compass heading and started out. By now it was at least 9:00 p.m. Ted found his legs

70

moved slowly and his pace was painstakingly slow but he was moving. After about one half-hour he came to the old narrow gauge railroad bed used by loggers at the turn of the century. Small locomotives pulled logging trains right on this bed he was crossing. When the logging in this area was done, the tracks and ties were picked up and taken to the next logging job. Ted was pleased that he found the old rail bed because it was where he expected it to be.

Another half-hour and Ted came to the fence for his farm. He crossed the fence and had a difficult time getting on his feet after rolling under it. He finally got on his feet. He leaned his .38-55 against the fence and stumbled toward home. Ted finally came over a hill and could see his house. Step by painful, stumbling step he came nearer and nearer to the house. His dog, Rex, saw the light from the lantern and he let out a series of loud excited yelps. Rex kept on barking but would not approach Ted. His barking caused Ann to come to a window. She could see Rex barking at something southeast of him. Ann went to another window so she could see out in that direction and saw the lanterns light but by that time Ted had collapsed so Ann could not recognize his inert form lying on the ground. She immediately knew someone carried that lantern there and it might be Ted. Ann put on a jacket and boots and told Jake and Lois she was going out to see what Rex was barking about.

Ann went out and made her way toward the lantern light. When she was about twenty-feet away she could see that there was someone lying the ground. She could not see the persons face as it was in the shadow caused by the light from the lantern. Ann approached closer and called Ted's name. Still no movement. She picked up the lantern and moved around to be able to see the face of this person stretched out on the ground. When she could see Ted's face, she could only see the bloody gash above his left eye as Ted was lying on his right shoulder with the right side of his face down in the snow.

Ann thought the clothes looked like what Ted wore when he left that morning. Ted's left shoulder was covered with blood and that is what Ann saw along with the bloody gash above his left eye. She bent down and rolled Ted on to his back and now she could see it was Ted. Ted recovered somewhat and Ann tried to comfort him. Ann helped Ted and he was able to sit up. Ann told Ted not to talk but to hold on to her and she would try to lift him up so they could get into the house. Ann and Ted tried but, Ted was so weak from loss of blood that, they could not get him up. About that time, a small person runs up and it was Jake. Ann told him that it was his dad and he is hurt. We need to get him up and into the house. "I can help," Jake said.

By now Ann knew they could not lift on Ted's left shoulder but maybe she could reach under Ted's coat and pull up on his belt. Jake could lift on Ted's right shoulder and maybe we can get him up. Ann got a hold on Ted's belt from behind him as he sat on the ground. Jake reached under Ted's right shoulder and on Ann's signal they all gave all they could and Ted was able to stand. He was very unstable but Ann and Jake had firm grips on him and were able to keep him from falling over.

Ted said he would try to walk toward the house. He took a step and with Ann and Jake holding him, he did not fall. Another slow step was taken and another and another. All at once, they could see light shining around them. Ann looked back and saw two lanterns rapidly approaching them from the southeast. Suddenly they heard the welcome words, **"Sheriffs deputies coming to help."**

In a short time two deputies ran up, one was carrying the .38-55. The gun was given to Ann and the two deputies took over holding Ted up. Ted was able to move a little faster and they reached the step leading up to the house. With much effort, Ted finally was in the house and was seated on a chair in the kitchen. Now Ann, Jake, Lois and the deputies could get a good look at Ted and he looked very scary. His face was bloody and his left eye was almost completely closed. Ted's left shoulder was covered with blood and there was a big hole on that shoulder of his jacket and windbreaker. His red windbreaker had two bullet holes in it.

The deputies thought that Ted should be taken to the hospital at Rice Lake. Besides that, they have an ambulance that can transport him there. Ann talked to Ted and asked if he agreed to go to the hospital and all he could do was look at Ann. She asked the deputies if they could use their communication system and order the ambulance as quickly as possible.

The call was made to the county dispatch system. The deputy told them that blood transfusion should be anticipated during transit. The deputy also asked for assistance as the squad car was parked on the town road to the east of Ted and Ann's home. Ted was now unconscious and his condition looked very serious. Ann covered him with blankets and got a small electric heater and turned it on near Ted.

Sunday Night, October 9, 1948

I got off the train from visiting Savannah and walked home to High Street. I walked in the door and Mom and Dad came to meet me. They were very happy to see me but I could see they were concerned about something. Mom put her arms around me and told me that Jean had died earlier this morning. That news hit me like a ton of bricks. I thought about Jean several times on the trip to Antigo and back. I knew that this moment would happen and I hoped I could handle it well, but I didn't. I looked at Mom and then hugged her and I cried. I left Mom and went to my room. I don't think I have ever been that sad anytime in my short life.

I came out of my room in a few minutes. Dad told me, "Jean passed away quietly. Howard was with her as were Sam and Carol. Jean's sister, Joan, was there also and she is the person that called us. She knows you were coming home today and if you want to be with Howard and the kids, you should feel free to come to Howard's home at Hayward this afternoon or evening." I said I wanted to go. Mom and Dad anticipated that I would want to do that so Mom had made a pan of brownies and a bunch of ham sandwiches to take to the family.

We arrived at Howard's home and went in. I saw Sam and Carol sitting in the kitchen. I went to both of them and gave them a long hug. They had been crying and we all cried for a short time. I sat down with them and we talked about our mother. I could tell that Sam and Carol really loved their mom and Jean really loved them. They both said it was going to be very difficult to go on without her. Several people were in the house and I met some of them but I wanted to leave as all of this was difficult for me to understand. I felt like I was not in control of my emotions and had a very strange feeling in my body. It may have been nerves but it must have been realization that my birth mother and I will be forever separated. That is strange since I only found out about Jean a short time ago. Apparently there is a very strong bond between myself and Jean. I hope this strange feeling goes away soon as it is making me feel sick.

Tuesday, October 11, 1948

Both yesterday and today, school seemed like a blur. I had a hard time being able to concentrate. Our freshmen football team played the Rice Lake freshmen and we lost 20 to 14. Darrell and I could only play two quarters. Our team played hard but Rice Lake had more players and they wore us down.

The funeral for Jean is Thursday at 11:00 a.m. The wake is Wednesday evening from 6:00 to 8:00 p.m. at a funeral home in Hayward.

Thursday, October 13, 1948

Football practice on Wednesday and today strictly concentrated on preparation for Rice Lake. The freshmen football season is finished but Darrell and I will continue through this game.

Coach Jenson put in a punt return for this game. It was set up so the punt return man, maybe me, will go to his right. After challenging the punter our linemen peel off to their right and come back and get a wall of blockers a few yards apart near the side line. The idea is that the punt return man be able to get behind this wall and the blockers will mow the Rice Lake players down.

Tony, a senior halfback and I caught all the punts and ran behind the wall. A lot depends on how the ball is kicked. Rice Lake had a very good punter that could punt long punts. This was what we wanted as it gave our team more time to set up the wall. The run back worked fine at least half the time.

The other special play put in was a screen pass off a fake punt. Ben was the regular varsity back and Darrell caught the screen pass on the left side of the formation. Rice Lake had a hard charging line that had blocked several punts this season. Coach Jensen said the play will really work if we are deep in our own territory and we have a long distance to go for a first down. Our punter was also our back up quarterback and was a good passer.

This was the last game of the season and it was at Spooner. It was also parents night so all Mom's and Dad's were invited to be introduced with their son and walk from the end zone to an area behind our bench. Rice Lake was undefeated and we had lost one game in the conference. If we could beat them we would be co-champions of the conference. We all wanted to beat Rice Lake and be co-champs. We all knew that Rice Lake had pretty much run rough shod through the other conference schools. They have about twice as many students as we do but we are confident that we can play with them and hopefully beat them.

Mom went to school on Wednesday and met with the principal to explain about Jean and the funeral. I did not go to school on Thursday until football practice. The principal and Coach Jensen met and coach agreed that it was alright for me to practice even though I had not been in school that day.

The visitation on Wednesday was very difficult. I found Sam and Carol as soon as I got to the funeral home.

We hugged and I could see both of them had been crying. I took their hands and the three of us walked up to see our mother. As we stood there, Carol put her arm around my waist. Sam did the same and I put my arms around both kids shoulders.

We talked very little and before long all three of us were crying. This was the saddest moment of my life. I felt sorry for myself, but I really felt sorry for Carol and Sam. Jean was the only mother they had and they were not prepared for life going on without their mother and it was scaring them. In a few minutes I felt someone's hands on my shoulder. It was Howard, my birth father, but the only father Carol and Sam had known. Very soon our Aunt Joan came and put her arms around all of us. Another aunt and uncle came up and joined our huddle by hugging us too. All of us were crying but amazingly, I felt a strong sense of belonging to these people in Jean's family.

Finally, the group separated and Carol said, "Mom sure looks beautiful. I am very sad she is gone but I am happy she is not in pain anymore. Good Bye, Mom." Both Sam and I thought Carol had said what we wanted to say, too. We both told Mom goodbye.

The funeral Thursday morning was at the funeral home. I had never been to a funeral before so Mom and Dad told me what to expect as we drove to the funeral. There were some songs and the minister read from the Bible. Finally, the casket was closed and I saw Jean for the last time. My eyes watered and I needed the handkerchief Mom had put in my jacket pocket. The casket was rolled out to a waiting hearse. The flowers were taken in the hearse and we got in our cars and once the hearse began moving, the cars with their lights on formed a long procession. We drove to the cemetery and up to the canopy over the freshly dug grave. The pallbearers carried Jean's casket to the waiting equipment to lower the casket into the ground.

This part was very hard for me to understand. Poor Jean was going to be put in this hole in the ground, covered with dirt and a headstone will be added to mark her final resting place. I suppose that this is the way it has to be but for poor Jean it just was very hard for me to understand.

The family was gathered under the canopy beside Jeans casket. Howard wanted me to sit by Sam and Carol. I held Carol and Sam's hand during the service. When it was finished, Howard asked, "Would the three of you like to take a rose out of the bouquet of flowers and put it on your mother's casket?" We did this and immediately we all cried. Finally Howard urged us back to the cars. We went to a restaurant that had been set up to serve a lunch to the family and friends that attended the funeral. Apparently, this is a custom that helps family and friends handle the mourning that they go through. I can tell you that I certainly am mourning but all the people gathering seems to help me recover from the shock of losing my birth mother. Mom and Dad were very kind and consoling to me.

After the game, Friday, October 14, 1948

School was difficult today and I just could not concentrate on my classes. My mind wandered to thoughts about Carol and Sam. Jean seems to be on my mind and I can't seem to stop thinking about her. I have to get over the fact that Jean is lying in a casket buried deep in the ground.

There was a huge crowd at the game tonight. It began to rain in the first quarter, but people kept coming. Rice Lake was a tough team. They had two good runners but our defense made adjustments so the Rice Lake runners had a hard time getting yards. They did score a touchdown in the second quarter so were ahead 7 to 0 at halftime.

In the third quarter, Rice Lake intercepted a pass and ran it back for a touchdown. Rice Lake 14, Spooner 0. On the kickoff, the wet ball bounced on the wet ground and Tony finally got control of it and was tackled on our seven yard line. Three running plays and we got it out to the thirteen yard line. Fourth down and Coach Jensen called for the screen pass from the fake punt. Darrell got sent in with the punt team. The play went just like we practiced. Rice Lake stormed in looking to block this desperate punt.

Darrell caught the pass and his blockers led the way and took out the two remaining defenders. Darrell ran eighty-seven yards for a touchdown. Now it is Rice Lake 14, Spooner 7.

Fourth quarter, late in the game and Rice Lake is forced to punt. Tony had been hurt and I had taken his place in the fourth quarter. The punt was long and it was still raining so the ball was wet and I nearly caught it, but then it dropped to the ground in front of me. I managed to pick it up quickly. The punt return to the right was called so I started right and got around the first man and was able to get behind the wall of blockers. Our guys picked off the Rice Lake guys and I ran down behind them all the way for a sixty-seven yard touchdown. The extra point was good and the game was tied at 14-all. Both teams struggled in the mud but that is how the game ended. Rice Lake is 5-0-1 and Spooner is 4-1-1. So Rice Lake wins the conference championship and Spooner is in second place.

Many of the varsity players came up to Darrell and me after the game and thanked us for being a part of the varsity team. We both felt good about that. 'Rough', 'Tough' and Joe were standing by the twenty yard line and were going crazy as I ran by them. After the game they waited for me until after I showered. I asked Darrell to come with us and we walked downtown and went to the Burger Barn and had a hamburger and a malt. The place was crammed with kids including several football players. Darrell and I got lots of pats on the back as everyone seemed really excited about the football game. Joe stayed overnight with me as he rode his bike to the game and it was dark and dangerous to ride his bike home. The five of us talked about going hunting Saturday. Joe said he would have to find out if his dad needed help, otherwise he could go with us.

Late Saturday, October 15, 1948

Joe had to help his dad in the later afternoon so the five of us hunted across the railroad tracks not far from Joe's home. We had shotguns and were hunting for partridge and rabbits. We did get four partridge and one rabbit. Joe had to be home by 2:00 P.M. so we were through hunting. Four of us got a partridge but we drew straws for the rabbit first so each of us had some game.

I wondered how Sam and Carol, my brother and sister, were getting along so I called to see if I could talk to them. They both were home and had some relatives and friends there but they were happy that I called. They did not go to school on Friday but will start again on Monday. We talked about lots of things and even though I could hear a sadness in their voice, they seemed happy. I am still feeling sadness whenever I think of Jean, Howard, Sam & Carol. I wrote a letter to Savannah, a project that I had put off because of the involvement with the funeral, plus I was struggling with what I would tell Savannah about Jean, Howard, Sam & Carol.

Late Monday, October 17, 1948

My involvement with my classes seemed more normal. Last week was just like a blur. I just laid around Sunday and I think that was good for me. I even slept in the afternoon. Today after school we handed in our football gear. This was a happy time as it was good to be with the varsity guys again. Coach Jensen was very friendly and thanked Darrell and me for helping out. He told us that he was looking forward to next year when both of us and several of the other freshmen teammates will have a crack at the varsity team. He told us to work hard and get a job that requires us to work hard.

Basketball practice starts next week and I am planning to try out even though I am not very good at it. I need to write some more on my story, *The Mob and the Deer Hunter.*

The deputy told Ann, "Another deputy and myself followed Ted's tracks right from home. We found where he had been wounded on the big ridge almost directly east of your place. We found lots of blood and could see where Ted ran toward the south. We found where he got behind

79

a small pile of dirt and shot at something, probably the person that wounded him. He continued south and then we found another set of tracks join his. This person was losing blood and was dragging one leg. We found where this other person stopped and shot at least once so Ted may have been hit again. We continued on a few hundred feet, and found where Ted was wounded again. The other man continued to follow Ted's tracks but now two other sets of tracks joined. We continued and after some distance we came upon a dead man."

"There was some confusion around the dead man. Did the men following him shoot him? Our lantern light did not allow us to see very far. Finally we saw a set of tracks come near the man and then went back the way they came. Other tracks led toward a spruce swamp and when we got closer we could see where a fire had burned part of two downed trees. There still was heat where the fire had been. The tracks led into the swamp and we found a spot where Ted must have waited for the man that was following him. The fire may have attracted him and Ted must have been able to shoot him," the deputy continued.

"We followed the tracks of three men, one of which was Ted's. All at once we heard many gunshots, deep pitched and very rapid. We had never heard any shooting like that and it was a long distance away. A few minutes later was another burst of several shots." The deputy said, "We were following the tracks when there was yet another burst of shots but right as the shots ended there was a rifle shot. We continued following the tracks when we could see a light coming toward us. We shut our lanterns off and waited because we thought the person with the light was probably following the tracks that they made following Ted."

"We watched the light get closer and closer. I was on one side of the tracks and the other deputy was on the other side and we were standing behind trees." He continued, "Finally, the man was about sixty to seventy feet away and we told the man to halt as we wanted to ask him some questions. He put his lantern down and brought up a Tommy

Gun and started shooting at my partner. I began shooting with my handgun. One of my shots hit the man and he died. My partner had been hit in the shoulder and upper leg and was bleeding badly. I had already called dispatch and asked for backup to come in from the town road. I used the other mans lantern and attended to my partner. The leg wound was bleeding profusely so I took his belt and cut off part of my shirt and wadded it up and put it on the wound. I put the belt around his legs and over the wadded up shirt over the wound. I pulled the belt as tight as I thought it should be. I used my knife to put a hole in the belt to keep the tension on the wound. The deputy held his hand on his shoulder wound and was in severe pain."

"About this time I heard a whistle off in the distance. I took out my whistle and blew several long blasts. It was answered so I used my walkie-talkie to contact the whistle blower. It was the sheriff with two other deputies and they were about three hundred yards away."

The deputy continued, "I told the sheriff about the shooting of the deputy and he needed immediate medical care. The sheriff said he would call dispatch and order an ambulance to pick up by our vehicles on the town road. It took about fifteen minutes before the sheriff and the other deputies reached us. The injured deputy could slowly walk with assistance of the sheriff and deputy. The three of them followed their trail back out to the town road."

"I had explained everything I knew about Ted being wounded. Now there were two dead men in these dark November woods and we still had not found Ted. All the shooting by the Tommy Gun off in the distance worried us and we wondered if Ted had indeed been shot. The sheriff told me to take one of the deputies and follow Ted's track. The sheriff picked up the Tommy Gun and took that as evidence. Lanterns were lit and our group split up. We followed Ted's track and the rest took the wounded deputy and headed to the town road."

Late Saturday, October 22, 1948

After breakfast, Mom, Dad and I sat around the table and talked about the recent events in my life as well as theirs. There is no doubt that my world was shaken since we learned about Jean and her family. Mom and Dad have been very, very supportive of me and have not tried to influence my thinking. They truly do love me and I love them. Recent events have shown me that this is my home and my family and if I wanted to get to know my new found family they will do whatever I would like them to do. There is no doubt that I intend to continue to be a part of this family and will try hard to help my mom and dad feel that they have done a wonderful job of supporting me.

Dad had the day off so I helped him put storm windows on the house. Several storm windows needed new putty before they could be put up. We finished by early afternoon and we took our shotguns and hunting gear and headed to the logging trails that Dad thought were going to have lots of partridge near them. It was a beautiful fall day, 65° F., sunny and not windy. The leaves were falling and many leaves have already fallen so hopefully we will be able to see the 'thunderbirds' when they fly.

We start down a logging road and Dad suggested that one of us go about twenty-five to thirty yards off the road and follow it. This will allow us to cover more territory and flush birds toward the other hunter. I volunteered to go off the road. Dad told me to walk slowly and if I came to an opening, I should stop about two or three steps before I step into the opening. I should pause for fifteen to twenty seconds and then step in and get ready for a bird to flush. I tried this and for the most part it really works. Apparently, by pausing for a short while makes the partridge nervous and when a hunter moves they will fly.

By this time it was nearly dark, and we went back to the car. Dad shot five birds and took eight shots. I shot five birds and took only seven shots. My practice during the winter by raising my empty gun and pointing at a target is definitely working. Partridge are very tasty and maybe Mom will bake some for supper on Sunday. The return trip to High Street was very pleasant. Dad is fun to be around and has been a good teacher to develop my fishing and hunting skills. Dad is very patient with me and gives me plenty of freedom to do things I want but will help or guide me, if needed.

After supper, I got a call from Savannah. Her main message was that her dad, Elon had gotten four tickets for the Green Bay Packers playing the Los Angeles Rams and 'Crazy Legs' Hirsch. "We would like to invite you and your dad to come to Antigo and ride with us to Green Bay for the game. The game is Sunday, November 6th at 12:00 noon. Maybe your mom can ride along and visit with my mom while we are at the game," she said.

I asked Savannah to hold on and I asked Mom and Dad if we could do what Savannah suggested. Dad checked his schedule and he had that Sunday off. It didn't take long for them to agree and to count on us to come to Antigo and then my dad and I would go on to Green Bay with Elon and Savannah.

Sunday, October 23, 1948

Mom fixed four partridge for supper. They were great! They are mostly white breast meat but the dark meat of the legs is also good. We have to be careful not to bite down on a lead pellet. Mom also fixed a wonderful apple pie using apples from our tree in the back yard. Mom reminded me that the dahlia bulbs needed to be dug and put in the basement when they are dry. I need to do this before the ground freezes.

In the afternoon, I rode my bike to Joe's house and found him helping his dad build a small barn for sheep. They were putting siding on so Joe said, "Grab a hammer and help me nail siding on." Joe's dad cut the siding to length and Joe and I nailed it on. As we went higher we needed to rig up a scaffold of sorts to reach up to the eaves. The ends had peaks and that required a more substantial scaffold until we got near the top and then Joe could work from a ladder to nail the siding on.

I asked Joe's dad what kind of sheep they would be getting. He said they will buy thirteen crossbred ewes and will buy a Dorset ram to breed the ewes. This ram has curled horns and could come after anyone that gets in the pen with the sheep. The breeding will be done so lambs are born in the middle of March and later. Joe is not going out for basketball mostly because he has not played much and doesn't think he would be any good at it. I told him, "You are one of the biggest boys in the freshman class and are certainly one of the strongest. If it is OK with your mom and dad, you could try it and if it is not going good and you don't feel you are making progress, you can drop out. No one will think much about it. But if you like it and are able to play pretty well you could help our team. 'Rough', 'Tough' and Darrell are going out and so am I. If you are interested, talk to your mom and dad. I can tell you that I would like to play basketball with you. I don't know if I can make the team but I am going to try out." Good night.

Late Tuesday, October 25, 1948

Two practice sessions for the freshmen basketball team and I am still on the team. Coach Jones is our basketball coach and all of the football kids really like him and are happy he is our coach. We don't do up-downs, but we run lots of sprints. We run and run so I can bet that we will be in shape. Joe is out for the team! He is big and strong and can really rebound. There are about twenty-five boys trying out and the coach told us that no one will be cut. We can only dress fifteen players for each game. It looks like a slow developing boy could work his way on to the team that plays other schools.

At Tuesdays practice Coach Jones had us all do the vertical jump. Each of us took a piece of chalk and reached as high as we could and made a mark on a painted board.

Next we jumped and made a mark with the chalk as high as we could reach. A measurement of the distance between the marks is the players vertical jump. Mine was twenty-six inches. Joe was twenty-five inches and Jim and Jed were both twenty-three inches. This was very interesting. Apparently some of us have more spring in our jump than others.

Friday Afternoon, October 28, 1948

My classes at school are going fine. My grades are good. Basketball is lots of running and drills. We have scrimmaged some and Darrell, Joe and I have played together. So far Jim and Jed are on the team we scrimmage against. I am playing a forward, Joe is a center and Darrell is a guard.

I have thought about my newly found brother and sister often in the past few days. I have an idea and want to talk to Mom and Dad after supper.

Dad has to work tomorrow and what I wanted to do was see if Sam would want to come to our house and I could take him into the Beaver Brook Wild Life Area. Mom would have to go to their house in Hayward to pick him up and Mom could take him home. I talked this over with Mom and Dad and they thought it would be alright to call and find out if Sam is interested and if it is alright with Howard. I called Sam and he wanted to go with me. He talked to Howard and it was alright with him too. See you in the morning.

Saturday, October 29, 1948

Mom and I went to pick up Sam in Hayward. I talked to Carol and told her I didn't know if she wanted to tramp around the woods all day. She agreed that she would not have much interest in doing that. She was going to spend some time at Aunt Joan's house.

My plan was to have Mom drop us off at the Cranberry Marsh and we would work our way toward my old campsite. From there we would go to the sluice dam, beaver pond and other places of interest. Mom was going to pick us up by 4:30 p.m. where the Wild Life Road crosses the railroad tracks. Mom had packed sandwiches for both of us and we each had a bottle of pop. The day was cool but bright and sunny. Many of the leaves had fallen and we had no guns with us.

Mom dropped us off by Little Dove and Walking Bear's quarters. I didn't know if they were still here yet or if they had left for Alabama. I was pretty sure the cranberry harvest was finished. I went to the door and knocked and Little Dove opened the door and when she saw me she came and gave me a big hug. I introduced Sam to her and she immediately went inside and came back out with a rabbit foot for Sam. I told her that Sam was my brother and explained about Jean, Howard and Carol. I told Little Dove that I was going to take Sam to all the places I had explored or discovered this past summer. Little Dove told me that Walking Bear had about two days work left and then they will catch a train to Alabama. Little Dove wanted us to stay but we were able to convince her that we had to leave. She gave each of us a big hug and we headed to the edge of the cranberry marsh where I explained how the beds were flooded from the reservoir to protect the berries from frost. Also flooding occurred when the berries were being harvested.

We walked north on the road to the bridge over Beaver Brook. I told Sam that the stream started in a lake about one mile south of the bridge and then runs about three and one-half miles in a northwesterly direction before it flows into the Yellow River. I told Sam about the three spring fed pools a little east of the bridge and told him about catching many nice trout, but releasing all of them. Sam had never fished trout but he had caught bass, pan fish and two northern pike.

We followed the stream as it flowed northwest. Sam was impressed by the beauty of the area. There are many large white pines by the steep banks of Beaver Brook. When we reached the big pine hole we sneaked up on it by crawling on our bellies and peeked over the bank to see if we could see trout. A cloud covered the sun and, for a brief time, we could see without the reflection on the water. I did spot a nice two pounder right below us and pointed it out to Sam. We continued downstream and I pointed out several holes that all produced trout this past summer.

We left the stream and headed to the beaver pond. Sam was amazed by the beaver dam. He had never seen a beaver dam, or a beaver, and he spent a fair amount of time examining the beaver dam. He concluded that the beaver is an industrious animal. We went around the south side of the pond so I could show Sam the sticks leading out to the edge of the deep spring hole producing the large stream of water flowing from the pond. I told about having the big trout up to me and was just reaching out with the net when it gave a mighty thrash and got free.

We headed up the hill toward the east and found the trail that leads toward Dick's old house. I told Sam about meeting Dick and Joe and watching them fish. I told about the 'bug' that Dick's family had and that they have moved to a different home about two miles away and are now living in the Shell Lake School District. As we walked along the trail, Sam asked who owns this land? I explained that it is owned by all of us and the Wisconsin Conservation Department manages it. Nearly all of the Beaver Brook stream is included in the wildlife area.

We followed the trail to the dirt road by Dick's old house. We were standing looking at the house when we heard a vehicle approach from the south. We stepped into the woods and watched the vehicle. It was Dick's bug and it was pulling a small trailer. Sam was amazed at the bug as he had never seen one before. Apparently, Dick's family was still moving some of their possessions and since this was a Saturday the kids didn't have to go to school and could help.

We headed back to the west on the trail. I told Sam about Dick waiting in these woods for a buck to come and eat acorns. When it did, Dick shot it. We got to the point on the trail where we could look through the tree tops toward the west and see the buildings of the farm on the hilltop that overlooks the valley of the Beaver Brook stream.

We headed to the south and in a few minutes found the site of the possible old hunting camp. Sam was impressed that long ago someone built a cabin here but now very little evidence remains. We headed back to the trail and continued down the hill and we could see the beaver pond off to our right. We walked to the southeast edge of the pond and stood and watched for a few minutes. Here came a beaver swimming near shore and only about thirty feet from us. There wasn't much we could see except its nose and the top of its head. I told Sam to clap his hands over his head and shout. He did and the beaver immediately brought its tail out of the water and slapped the water with a loud 'whap' and then dove out of sight. **Wow**, was Sam's exclamation!

We continued to the northeast part of the pond and left the pond and headed toward the site of the old logging camp. As we headed toward the old camp, Sam wondered how I knew where it was in this huge woods. I explained that I was following blaze marks I had made with my knife. I showed the next one to him and told him to look on the opposite side of the tree and he found another blaze mark. He said that must be so we can find our way back from the old camp.

We found the place where the old logging camp was and Sam was impressed. They had just studied about logging in the Hayward area about the turn of the century. He saw pictures of these old log buildings that the men lived in during the winter when the logging was done. He asked me if I thought any of our relatives could have worked here. I do know that many old time families in the area came because of the logging and stayed around after the logging ran out so it is possible that our great-grandfathers may have worked here or in other camps. We decided to see what kind of sandwiches Mom packed so we sat down and ate peanut butter and jelly on Mom's fresh homemade bread.

Sam seems like a bright, interesting boy. Physically he can easily keep up with me and appears to be quite athletic.

He is in the seventh grade now and likes to play football at home and at school. He said it is completely unorganized but fun. I told him about my football endeavors and he seemed impressed. He was especially impressed that I played on the varsity team this fall. He likes to play basketball, too, and he and a few boys living nearby play once in a while. He said he likes school and gets good grades, mostly A's.

He gets along good with Howard and he and Jean were really good about supporting the school and visiting during parent-teacher conferences. He said he is about the fastest boy in their physical education class. He said, "I really like to read and my favorite book is *The Call of the Wild.* I recently found a book called *Wild Animals I Have Known.*" He said. "One story is about 'Krag' a mountain sheep out in British Columbia. Another is about 'Lobo' a huge wolf in Texas. There are other stories but these are the ones I like the best." I told him, "I have read *Call of the Wild* but not *Wild Animals I Have Known.*" Sam said he will lend it to me when we take him home. I really like Sam and he seems to like me. Having a brother is certainly new to me but I am liking it.

We finished our sandwiches and got up to leave when Sam said, "I can picture what went on here, lots of men working hard during the day. Then coming back to camp and sitting down to big meals made by the cook. They had to dry out wet work clothes in the bunk house. Horses and oxen were cared for and new shoes put on them when needed. The blacksmith was a very important man in a logging camp. We learned about that in school and now I can stand here and imagine what went on right around where I am standing."

I told Sam to see if he could lead us back the way we came. It took a couple of false starts but he found the blaze marks and led the way and only one time ran off the marks. When he realized he had not seen a mark for awhile I told him to hang his cap on a bush where he stopped, go back the way he came by following tracks made in the foliage and grass. When you get back to a blaze mark, see where you went wrong, find the next blaze and break a small branch down but not off, go retrieve your hat and continue on. Sam got along just fine. We came to the edge of a steep hill and the blaze marks went down and I called a halt to our travels as we were by the remains of the cabin made by the trapper, Frank Steffan.

I took out my flashlight from my backpack and we crawled under the giant oak tree that had fallen over the doorway to the cabin built into the hill. We got inside and used the flashlight to see the inside. Sam was really impressed. We didn't stay long and once we were back outside I told Sam about Frank Steffan who trapped starting in the winter of 1929 and continued until 1932. Dry conditions, fire and the depression brought an end to Frank living here. He got a job with the railroad and was killed when a train hit the handcar he was riding on during a storm. The county took his forty acres in 1934 because he had not paid his taxes for the past three years. I will finish writing about our Saturday tomorrow. Good night.

Sunday Morning, October 30, 1948

It is a rainy day. I will finish my story about my day with brother Sam.

Sam and I left the trappers cabin and followed the blaze marks to the west side of the beaver pond. We scared up several ducks as we approached the pond. We continued a few yards to Beaver Brook and a few yards down stream to the remains of the sluice dam. We stood and looked at the four 12' x 12' timbers that spanned the stream here. I asked Sam what he thought he was looking at. He looked at the surrounding hills and said, "It doesn't look like it was a bridge." We walked on one of the timbers to get to the west side of the stream. Finally Sam said, "I wonder if it was part of some sort of dam at one time?" I told him that he apparently was right. A dam could have been built on these timbers and during the spring snow melt the dam would have held back a huge lake of water, five to six feet deep. Logs would be piled up downstream and when the dam was opened a huge surge of water flowed downstream and the logs were rolled in and sent downstream to a saw mill. The stream would have been cleared of branches, etc. that could stop logs and cause a log jam. Loggers with long pike poles were positioned in trouble spots to keep these pine logs moving.

I asked Sam to compare the size of the Beaver now as compared to when we were on the bridge. I told Sam about the great trout holes around the timbers and those nearby a little downstream. I went a little to the west of the sluice dam and came to the little spring hole that Dad and I caught the giant trout in. I told Sam about catching the fish and releasing it in Beaver Brook. When I told him it weighed seven and three-quarters pounds, his eyes got very wide.

We then headed south toward my summer camp site. When we got to the beautiful grove of tall white pines, Sam said, "This is a cool place." I showed him where my tent was and where Earl pitched his tent. I told Sam about Earl and about his problem of adjusting to life with his injured leg and other problems. I told him about the day he went looking for the old logging camp and got confused and thought he was under attack like he was on Iwo Jima.

I told about the three half-grown red fox pups that came into camp many times. They eventually took food out of my hand. Sam asked if they were still around and I said they may be but more than likely they have dispersed. He wanted to go to the den and look for them. Before we went, I told him about the family of saw-whet owls. We looked up in the pine trees but could not see any. We started off to look for the fox den when, all at once, we heard the screechy-scratchy call of a saw-whet owl coming from a lower limb of an elm tree by the stream. We slowly walked toward the little owl and finally were about six feet away from the owl as it looked at us and from time to time swiveled its head to look around. I told Sam to move closer and see if he could touch the owl. He finally was able to touch one of its claws but then it moved away. We watched the owl for several minutes and then continued on our search for the three foxes.

We found the fox den but no foxes. We continued south and came to the little stream that flows under the railroad trestle. We came to the little pool where I was sitting when the ten-point buck came and got a drink a few feet from me. Sam was amazed. We followed the stream upstream, finding several places where the stream disappeared under the matting of tree roots and shrubs. As we looked, Sam remarked that this was a beautiful spot, quite unusual. I told him that the water comes from a spring in a swamp the other side of the railroad tracks.

We started back toward the summer campsite. This route took us near the fox den so we checked it out as we came to it. Low and behold, one of the fox pups had been resting near the den and now it came slowly walking toward us. I told Sam to stay back and I slowly approached the fox, softly talking. It stayed where it was and I sat down about fifteen feet away and held out my hand. The fox looked around but in a few minutes got up and walked near me. It smelled my hand and then gave it a lick! It then stepped back and sat down. It walked off about ten feet, laid down and fell asleep. Sam could hardly believe his eyes!

We continued back to the campsite. I explained that the railroad track was just up the hill and Dad drove a large slow moving train that he could drop off food, clothes and other things. Sam asked if maybe next summer he and I could camp and fish at this spot. I told him that it may be possible. Howard and my folks would have to give their approval.

By now there was just enough time to visit one more place before we walk to where Mom was going to pick us up. In a few minutes from the campsite, we came to the tangle of blown over trees and Joe Pachoes winter home for part of the winter of 1929-30. I dug out the flashlight and we went into the tangle. I pulled the carved branch out of the ceiling and showed the carving with the dates on it.

I told Sam the story about Joe Pachoe, what my dad had heard about him and that he may have seen him once. We hiked west to the railroad track and then walked the tracks toward the meeting place with Mom. We heard a diesel train whistle south of us and in a few minutes here came a freight train. We found a place to step off the tracks a decent distance. The engine and cars approached and then I realized that Dad may be driving that train and he was! We waved and he waved back and he hit a very short blast on the whistle. We continued walking the track and I told Sam about meeting Savannah and her family on the Beaver this summer. I told him about her tremendous fishing skills and that we got to be good friends. In fact, this coming Sunday, Mom, Dad and I will be driving to Antigo then Savannah, her dad, my dad and I will drive to Green Bay to see the Green Bay Packers play the Los Angeles Rams.

Mom was waiting to pick us up. Dad had given her a short blast on the whistle also. Mom drove right to Sam's house without stopping at our place. Mom visited with Sam on the way. Mom could tell that Sam really enjoyed the day and admired his big brother for the way he had spent the summer. Sam had told me that he wanted to spend more time exploring and fishing on Beaver Brook. When we got to Sam's house, Sam ran in to the house and came back out with the book he was going to lend me. Howard came out with Sam and thanked me for taking Sam into the wilderness. Sam already told him that he had a wonderful time. It took two and one-half hours to write this part of my diary. Good night.

Late Sunday, October 30, 1948

I am going to write more on my story, ***The Mob and the Deer Hunter.***

"The other deputy and I followed the trail of tracks assuming one of the tracks was Ted's." He said, "After a few hundred yards we came to the abandoned house we found where the guy with the Tommy Gun blazed away at the house. Some tracks led toward the small barn and more

shots were fired at it."

"We went into the house with our guns drawn but didn't find anyone inside. The back door was open so we went outside and a few feet away laid another dead man. By now we figured that Ted must have shot this guy and since we did not see the Tommy Gun, the man that we shot on the trail must have picked it up and left before Ted shot him too."

"We did not find any lantern but we saw where one was set down in the snow. Maybe the man we shot on the trail picked it up, but maybe Ted did. We called Ted's name and circled the house looking for tracks. There were so many tracks we could not determine anything. We stopped and thought. Ted was deer hunting and most hunters carry a compass. Maybe Ted picked up the lantern and now he could read his compass and started for home. He also could be lying dead somewhere."

"I got out my compass and from what I could figure, we would have to go northwest in order to get to Ted's place. We went to the northwest corner of the house and looked at the compass and started walking. We had not gone very far and we found Ted's tracks heading northwest. We found little traces of blood so we were certain it was Ted's tracks. We followed them right to Ted, you and the kids. I am going to go out and start my car and turn my red lights on so the ambulance will know where to go. I will call dispatch and tell them to tell the ambulance driver about the red lights."

Ann had spread blankets on the sofa and the deputy helped Ann get Ted onto the sofa. Ted was very weak and nearly unresponsive but he did manage to tell the deputy, "I saw a man shot and probably killed at the bottom of the big ridge east of here. Someone saw me watching and he shot me." The deputy immediately called the sheriff and told him what Ted told him. There was a pause but then the sheriff told the deputy, "Stay with Ted at all times, take Ann with you and I will send a deputy to Ted's house to stay with the kids. Apparently the mob must have killed someone and are very willing to silence Ted. Be alert to anyone approaching Ted in his room at the hospital. We will try to find the dead guy in the morning."

In a few minutes, two deputies cars pulled into Ted and Ann's place. One of the cars was the spare squad car left on the town road. In a few minutes the ambulance drove in and the attendants quickly assessed Ted's condition. Ted had lost a great amount of blood but the crew did not have blood on the ambulance but they did give Ted an intravenous solution to replace lost fluids due to the gunshot injuries. Ted was put on a stretcher and loaded into the ambulance. The deputy told Ann, "Go with Ted as the two deputies will stay with the kids. When you need to come home, one of us will take you. Your kids will be well cared for and so will you and Ted."

The ambulance ride to Rice Lake was agonizing for Ann. Ted was sleeping and the attendants felt Ted was stabilized for now. Ann was not so sure. Ted was a young strong man in good physical condition but he lay quietly in front of her. She was very worried that Ted was injured very badly. By now it was past midnight. Ted had been injured for about ten hours. He also must have been under great stress as he was being pursued by those men.

The ambulance arrived at the hospital and Ted was wheeled into the emergency room where two doctors and several nurses quickly attended to him. Ann and the deputy waited outside and about one and one-half hours later the two doctors came to Ann and told her, "Ted is resting. He received three pints of blood. The wounds were sewed up and dressed. Ted has a fever from an infection he got from his wounds. We gave him some medicine and that should control the infection. Ted is very weak and he will probably sleep most of the day. We will be monitoring his vital signs carefully." Ann and the deputy were taken to Ted's room.

Ann worried about many things. Will Ted recover? Will he be able to work like he did or will he be handicapped? Will the kids be alright? Who will take care of milking the cows and feeding the animals? How will we pay for all of this?

Late Tuesday, November 1, 1948

Basketball practice is at 7:00 p.m. this week. With only one gym, the varsity, junior varsity and freshmen teams practiced at a variety of times. My feet hurt from all the running, stopping and turning. It seems that I am getting blisters and callous on my feet where I had not had them before. All of us on the team are complaining about sore feet. So far Coach Jones is making us run and do wind sprints with no let up. We all hope he will lighten up a little but I don't intend to do anything but give my best effort. We do shoot plenty of free throws and one of the managers keeps track of percentage of free throws we make. If we fall below seventy percent it means staying after practice and shooting up to three rounds of ten each. If we make seventy percent or higher on the first round of ten we are done. If not, we shoot the next ten and if needed, we shoot the last group of ten. Then no matter how lousy we do, we are finished with practice for that day. Coach Jones tabulates all this free throw information so we all have a percentage at all times. Sometimes he will refer to us by our free throw percentage other than our name. I am right around seventy-one to seventy-two percent. One player, Alex, shoots eighty-one percent and many of the players are less than seventy percent.

We scrimmage nearly every practice and the managers keep shot charts of where a shot is taken from and if it is made. Other managers keep rebound records. Coach Jones processes all this and we know it will help him decide who will play. We do think that nearly everyone will get some playing time, especially the fifteen that dress for games.

Last night I started reading the book my brother Sam lent me. It had several short stories and the first one was about a mountain sheep that lived in the Canadian mountain range called the Kooternay range in British Columbia. This ram got to be old and had massive curled horns. He was a legend and many hunters tried to get him including an old Trapper and hunter called Scotty. He had tried to shoot this ram called Krag for many years.

Finally, Scotty packed his bedroll and knapsack and vowed to stay after Krag until he got him. Krag and Scotty knew each other well. The ram took off for a distant part of the mountain. He knew the range of Scotty's gun and stayed at least six hundred yards ahead but always in sight of each other. This chase went on for nearly a month and more than a hundred miles. They were nearly back to where the chase began.

Scotty came up with a plan. He would make camp where he could slip out of his bedroll and get down in a valley. The night before he gathered up many willow branches and near dawn he put them in his bedroll so Krag would think he was still there. He slipped over the edge and into a valley that took him very near Krag's position.

Krag stood waiting for Scotty to begin the chase as Scotty carefully crept to within sixty yards of this magnificent animal. Krag might have seen him but the huge curl of his horn blocked his view. Up went the gun that never missed. Scotty nearly could not shoot his old adversary but in the end, Scotty's steady hand fired his gun. Scotty didn't want to look and maybe hoped he had missed, but he didn't. Scotty approached the body of Krag, his horns were even more massive than Scotty thought they were. Scotty had a sad, sick feeling as he looked down at Krag, lying dead on the ground.

Scotty had the massive head mounted. He kept it covered with a blanket and he would not show it to anyone. Scotty never hunted again and a couple of winters later a tremendous avalanche swept down on Scotty's cabin and Scotty was killed. The mounted head of Krag was unharmed and today hangs in a nearby museum.

After reading this story from the turn of the century, I had a sad feeling. Krag was a wild animal that had great survival skills and Scotty had tricked him. He crept up behind Krag and shot the ram without giving it a chance to escape. Scotty apparently felt he had not been fair with the ram. His reaction was about the only way he could honor his long time adversary. Some credit should go to Scotty for developing a plan and having the perseverance to trail the ram for a hundred or more miles.

Late Thursday, November 3, 1948

We had hard practices. We learned two out-of-bounds plays. My free throw average is seventy-three percent. Our first game is Thursday, a week from tonight. We will play the Barron freshmen. Darrell, Joe and I seem to play together most of the time. Sometimes we play with Jim and Jed and other boys. My feet seem to be getting better. The first varsity basketball game is Friday night when we play Ladysmith at Spooner. Coach Jones wants all of us to go to the game and sit together if we can. We should be there for the junior varsity game, too. On Sunday we go to Antigo and then to Green Bay. I really miss Savannah and am looking forward to seeing her and watching the Packers play the Rams.

Saturday, November 5, 1948

Jim, Jed and I went squirrel hunting with Jim's dad. We went to a large woods northwest of Spooner. We all had .22 caliber rifles. It was a sunny, cool day. Mom reminded me that the dahlia bulbs needed to be dug so I did that before I went hunting.

There were several large oak trees in the woods we were hunting in. Jed and I sat in a large grove of oaks. We sat quietly and watched the trees for any signs of squirrels. In a few minutes, two squirrels showed themselves on branches in the trees nearby. We just raised our guns and shot at the squirrels. Jed hit the one he was shooting at, but I missed mine. In the next two hours, I had better luck and shot three squirrels and Jed had four. Jim and his dad came to our location and each of them had four squirrels. We called it a day and headed home. I cleaned the squirrels and Mom cooked them for supper and they were very tasty.

Monday, November 7, 1948

We had a wonderful day! Mom, Dad and I drove to Antigo on Sunday morning. We left home at 4:00 a.m. and got to the Casey's house by about 7:30 a.m. We had a wonderful breakfast with the Casey's. Mom stayed with Kathy while the rest of us put on warm clothes and headed to Green Bay for the Packers game. It took a couple of hours to drive to Green Bay. Elon knew where the stadium was located which was on the east side of town at East High School.

We crossed the Fox River and had to wait for a ship to pass as the bridge was raised. Green Bay has several huge paper mills as well as many other industries. I could see huge piles of coal on the banks of the river. We arrived at the stadium and parked in a large lot near the field. Green Bay East High School is where the Packers play. There are huge wooden bleachers around the field but outside of the track. We got there early so we could watch both teams warm up.

I spotted Elroy 'Crazy Legs' Hirsch early on. He was a large guy and he raised his legs high as he ran. Elon said the Rams were favored but the Packers had been playing pretty good lately. By the time the game started, all the seats were filled and hundreds stood on the corners where there were no bleachers. We had good seats up about ten rows and on the west forty yard line on the north side of the field. It was a cool day and it was cloudy but there was no wind.

The Packers scored first on a long pass play. The Rams got the kickoff and moved the ball to mid-field. 'Crazy Legs' caught a swing pass on the right side. He sidestepped a Packer and then scored a touchdown on a long run. The score was tied at halftime, but the Packers recovered a fumble on the kickoff and scored in a few plays. In the fourth quarter, the Packers intercepted a Rams pass and had a long run back to the ten yard line. A few runs by 'Thunder Thornton' and the Packers scored again and led by the score of 21 to 7.

The Rams took the kickoff back to mid-field and steadily moved the ball and scored with about three minutes to play. The Packers connected on a long pass to the Rams fourteen yard line. Three plays and no gain so they kicked a field goal and now led 24 to 14 with less than a minute left in the game. The Rams ran a screen play for forty-five yards to the Packer seventeen yard line. There were forty-seven seconds left and the Rams threw that same swing pass to 'Crazy Legs' and he caught it and made cuts and using his stiff arm he scored a touchdown. Now there were thirty-nine seconds left and the score was Green Bay 24, Rams 21. The Rams tried an onside kick and the Packers were ready for it and made the recovery. The Rams held the Packers and used all of their timeouts so the Packers had to punt with twenty-three seconds left in the game. The punt was high and the Packers tackled the runner immediately. The Rams had no time outs left and twenty-one seconds to play. Everyone knew it was going to be a pass and the Packers were laying back. The play was a draw play to 'Crazy Legs'. He broke free of the lineman and was running freely in the Packers defense. Two or three Packers missed on tackles and it looked like 'Crazy Legs' would score but finally three Packers ganged up on him and stopped him on the four yard line. Time ran out and the Packers had pulled an upset as the Rams were undefeated. The fans went wild. That was some game!

As we made our way out of the stands, I could see 'Crazy Legs' coming toward his teams bench which was right in front of us. He came to pick up something near his team bench. I went up to the fence and said, "Hello, 'Crazy Legs'." I told him he played a great game. He came over to the fence and asked my name. I told him about reading of his training in the hills around Wausau. He said, "Yes, I did that and it really helped." I told him, "I did that in the woods around Spooner but I used a chunk of wood instead of a football." He laughed and told me, "Keep up your training. Maybe you could take my place on the Rams someday." He waved goodbye and I waved back. Super Wow!! 'Crazy Legs' seemed like a very nice guy. Imagine, taking time to talk to a nobody kid like me and he seemed to enjoy it. I can hardly believe it happened. Savannah, Elon and my dad were really impressed that I got to meet 'Crazy Legs' and talk to him. Several other people nearby were impressed that 'Crazy Legs' spoke to me like he did.

We headed back to Antigo and on the way Elon told us some of the history of the Packers. They were one of the original National Football League teams. The other original team left is the Chicago Bears that were the Staley Bears in 1919 when the NFL started. Other teams were from Duluth, Potsdam, Canton and others that all dropped out. Other teams took their places like the Steelers, Lions, Cardinals, Giants, Colts, Rams, Forty-Niners, and Eagles. So right now there are ten teams in the NFL. The Packers have won several world championships. Several years ago the team needed money so they sold shares of stock to ordinary people. They have no say in how the team is run but they can go to a yearly stockholders meeting. Lately there has been talk about the Packers building their own stadium.

Savannah and I had very little time to ourselves but we did hold hands as we sat in the backseat of Elon's car on the way back to Antigo. When we got to Antigo we had a lunch that Kathy had prepared and then we headed to Spooner. I shook Elon's hand and thanked him for arranging for the tickets to the game. "I really enjoyed it and having a chance to meet 'Crazy Legs' was wonderful. I really enjoyed the day with Savannah and you."

Late Thursday, November 10, 1948

Spooner freshmen 32, Barron freshmen 29. It was close but we won, thanks to Joe. He grabbed a lot of rebounds and scored ten points. Darrell scored eight points and I got five points. Coach Jones said he was happy with our play but I think we made plenty of mistakes. Anyway, we play Ladysmith next Thursday.

Late Saturday, November 12, 1948

Coach Jones really was upset with our play against Barron. We had a very hard practice and we really worked on man to man defense and rebounding. He showed us how to get inside position for rebounding. We had to block the opponent from getting near the basket. I like to rebound and I realize how important it is to our team.

Dad and I took our deer rifles to the rifle range to practice shooting and to see if our guns are sighted in properly. Dad has a bolt action .30-06 with open sights. I have a bolt action .30-30 that Dad had when he was younger. The gun is fairly light and easy to carry. It doesn't kick very hard when I shoot and it also has open sights. We shot at targets eighty yards away and both of us were able to hit the target consistently.

On the way back home we stopped at the sport shop and bought our hunting licenses and Dad bought a box of .30-06 cartridges, 150 grain bullets. Next Saturday is the opening day of deer season and we plan to hunt in the Beaver Brook Wild Life Area the first day at least. Dad only has to work on Tuesday and Wednesday during the season.

This afternoon I rode my bike to Joe's place to see if they had the sheep yet. Joe was not home but his mom said he was checking his traps across the railroad tracks down by the marsh. Joe had told me at school he was trapping muskrats so I went looking for him. It took awhile but finally I saw Joe out in the water working with his traps. Joe saw me and waved and told me to meet him on the south end of the marsh.

When we met, he came walking with four muskrats tied on twines over his shoulder. He had one more trap to check so he waded out to a runway and pulled up a trap with a muskrat in it. He reset the trap and we headed for home. Joe skinned the 'rats' and, with the skin side out, put the hides on stretchers to dry. Joe hopes to get two to three dollars per skin when he sells them this winter.

Joe said they have the sheep and we went to look at

them. They had a pen outside of the new barn that was built. The sheep seemed pretty calm and we walked in among them. I asked about the ram and Joe said they had him but we don't want him in with the ewes yet so he is in a pen in the big barn. We went to see the ram. Wow! He had a set of curled horns and looked like he wanted to get after us. Joe said he was a Dorsett breed and he will come after you if you are not careful. We plan to put him in with the ewes after Christmas.

Joe was planning to go duck hunting on a small lake north of his place and asked me to go with him, so off we went. I had no gun but I really didn't mind. I had never hunted ducks and was curious about it. We hiked to the lake and sneaked up on it by moving on our hands and knees through the grass on the south edge of the lake. We could hear some ducks quacking nearby and finally we could peek up enough to see them just a few yards away. Joe whispered and said he would rise up and when the ducks flew he would try to shoot one or two. He stood up with his gun ready. The ducks saw him and flew away. Joe had a pump shotgun with three 12 gauge shells in it. He fired all three rounds and two ducks fell in the water. One was not moving but the other was swimming in circles so Joe reloaded and shot it again. It stopped swimming. Joe gave me his gun and, since he had his hip boots on, he waded out and picked up one duck. The other duck was in deeper water and Joe could not reach it, but it was only about ten feet too far out. Joe came back to shore and said we had to find a stick or small tree to pull the duck close enough to reach. In a few minutes, we found a small dead tree standing, we pushed it over and Joe took it out in the lake and retrieved the duck. Both were mallards.

I told Joe that Dad and I had shot our rifles and bought our licenses. Joe and his dad were going to hunt across the railroad tracks in the Wild Life area. They also have land that relatives own and they will hunt on it. We both hope there is going to be snow by then.

Sunday, November 13, 1948

It is a cold, rainy day. I will write some more on my story, ***The Mob and the Deer Hunter.***

Ted slept and Ann tried to rest but found she could not. With the presence of the deputy, did the sheriff think these bad men will come to Ted's hospital room and try to finish the job? Would they try to silence her also since she would have seen whoever it was that tried to harm Ted. Finally it was morning. Ann realized that the cows would need milking and other chores done. She asked the deputy, "Could you contact the deputy that is staying with Jake and Lois, and see if they could contact our neighbor, Christ Olson, and tell him that Ted is badly hurt and will not be able to care for the animals at home, both this morning and tonight. Maybe longer. Also try to find out how Jake and Lois are getting along."

In a few minutes the deputy came into Ted's room and told Ann, "Jake and Lois are fine and one of the lady deputies will be with them all day as well as another deputy." Ann was relieved and finally got some sleep. Ted's vital signs remained stable but not as good as the doctors would like. The infection in Ted's body has not been controlled yet. The deputy returned and told Ann, "The deputies reached Christ Olson and he will do the chores today and for as long as needed. He wanted you to know that he and his wife will be thinking about you, Ted and the kids. And they said to stay strong."

About 10:30 a.m. the sheriff and another deputy came to Ted's room to talk to Ann. He was very kind and wanted Ann to know that they are working at sorting out all that had happened. "I can tell you that shortly after dawn, the deputies found the body of a man where Ted said he saw him get shot. There was no identification on the body. He had been shot several times. His body was removed and taken to the sheriffs office to try to identify this person, recover bullets and try to match them if we can. Fingerprints will be taken and we will find out who this person is. The bodies of

104

*the other three men have also been taken to our facility and
we will find their identity too. The state crime lab, with their
portable laboratory, is on its way here from Madison."*

*"We found an abandoned Cadillac on the town road
east of your place. It had an Illinois license plate and we
suspect it belonged to one of the men in our facility or they
at least drove it there. Also during the night another black
Cadillac with Illinois license plates with two occupants was
hit by a train on a crossing near Stone Lake. The car was
severely damaged and both men were killed. Both of these
vehicles have been removed to the county highway garage
and locked behind a secured fence in the building. The
bodies of the two men killed in the wreck have also been
taken to the sheriffs facility. The coroner has been contacted
and has been very busy."*

*"These two black Cadillac's appear to be the same
ones that had been seen in the area a week or ten days ago.
We had reports of several men, up to six, that were associated
with these cars. There may be other cars and other men
involved, but for now we think that these six dead men were
the only ones involved in this entire affair."*

*This news from the sheriff was somewhat comforting
to Ann. Maybe nobody will come after Ted now. What if
there are others that the sheriff does not know about or that
more may come looking for revenge or to try to silence Ted.
How much will all of this cost?*

Late Wednesday, November 16, 1948

There has been a lot of talk about deer hunting.
Many bucks have been seen running in places not normally
seen. The bucks are in the rut which means this is when the
bucks seek out the does and if the timing is right, breeding
is accomplished. Most fawns are born in May in this area.

With the opening day of deer season November 19th,
some bucks might be in the rut yet. This means that a lucky
hunter could have a buck run near enough for a shot. Bucks
expend a great amount of energy chasing after a doe and
fighting other bucks for breeding territory. In our forestry

class, we learned that during winters of deep snow the deer go into yards where hundreds of deer congregate in heavy, thick, evergreen forests. The food begins to be eaten up and amazingly some of the first deer to die are the large breeding bucks. Apparently they use up all of their stored fat during the rut so their food reserve is gone. We saw pictures of dozens of dead deer in these yards. Lately our winters have had very deep snow and the deer cannot move around easily. Because of the deep snow very little logging is done which is bad for the deer as they browse on the tops of trees cut down and they can walk on the logging roads.

Basketball practice this week is at 5:00 p.m. and we have had hard practices. There are a lot of rebounding drills and man to man defense. We all work on our shooting during the first part of our practice. My free- throw percentage is still seventy-three. Because my free throw percentage is seventy or higher, I only have to shoot ten free throws at the end of each practice. This week I have made twenty-three out of thirty free throws at the end of practice.

Friday, November 18, 1948

It snowed four inches today. Spooner freshmen basketball team 31, Ladysmith freshmen 29. This was a good team but we out rebounded them and we hit some good shots. They had two tall players that we had trouble stopping. No practice today and because Spooner schools are closed all of next week for deer hunting, there will be no practice for us. The gym will be open for players of all teams to go in and shoot on Friday.

The students are really excited about deer hunting. A few girls hunt but the boys do most of the hunting for deer. Some boys go to deer camp with their fathers, uncles and friends. Many of us do just like I will do. I will hunt with my dad and come home every night.

Tonight Dad and I get ready to head out in the morning well before it gets light. The knives are sharpened, back tag pinned on the back of our jackets, clothes and boots are readied, compass and fire starting kits are put in pants pockets.

Our guns are cleaned and oiled, ammunition is readied, gun cases are located and then it looks like we are all prepared. When I look at the pile of clothes that I will put on I am impressed. I wonder if that ten-point buck I saw come to get a drink has been fighting other bucks for breeding rights in his territory. I do know that bucks sometimes fight to the death and sometimes their antlers lock and eventually both will die. I am excited about being able to carry a gun and hunt this year. The last two years I went with Dad but I could not carry a gun.

Late Saturday, November 19, 1948

Today was a great day to hunt deer. Fresh snow and about 20° F. when we left home at 5:45 a.m. There was a slight breeze from the south. Dad and I parked near the railroad track and the Wild Life Road. We walked down the tracks toward the south and about 6:30 a.m. we left the tracks and went into the woods near Joe Pachoes tangle of downed trees. Our plan was to very slowly hunt our way south staying west of the stream.

We heard shooting by 6:45 a.m. but none was close by. By 7:00 a.m. I began to find a lot of deer tracks. Dad was about one-hundred yards to my right and closer to the tracks. He told me that we should go so slow that it may take thirty minutes to go the length of a football field. We would look for deer standing, bedded down or walking. We would need to listen, look and walk very quietly and be alert all the time.

By 10:00 a.m. I was about halfway between the sluice dam and my old campsite. All at once, I heard a shot on my right. It sounded very close and I thought it was Dad. I stayed very still and looked in the direction of the shot. Suddenly, three deer came toward me from the direction of the shot. I could not see antlers on any of them. After about ten minutes, I heard a low whistle that sounded like Dad. I decided that Dad wanted me to come to him.

In a few minutes, I saw Dad and he was standing very still. I approached closer and then I could see the curve of an antler above the snow. I finally got to where I could see a very nice eight-point buck lying dead by Dad. I was happy to see it wasn't the ten-point buck that I saw drinking water this summer.

Dad told me that the buck was following three does and had just crossed the railroad track. He watched for an opening and fired a shot at about sixty-five yards. The buck ran about fifty yards and dropped here. Dad said, "Now the work starts." He took his jacket off and got his hunting knife out of its sheath and started removing intestines, lungs and heart. When that job was finished he cleaned his hands in the snow and got out the metal tag with his back tag number on it. He attached that to one of the bucks hind legs. He got a rope out of his jacket and tied it around the bucks antlers which Dad estimated were about seventeen inches wide. One tine had the tip broken but otherwise it was a beautiful rack.

We decided that we better drag the deer to the car and take it home before we continue hunting. Dad rigged the rope so each of us would have an end that we could tie a small piece of wood on to keep our hand from slipping off the rope. With both of us pulling, the buck slid along quite well on the snow. However, we were almost a mile from the car. Finally, we reached the car and we opened the trunk and put the buck in. When we got home we hung the buck in a tree in the back yard. That was not an easy job, but we got it done. Dad said we can skin it and cut it up tonight.

By this time it was 2:00 p.m. and Dad said we would go to the woods west of town that one of his engineer friends own. Dad explained that I would stand on the southwest edge of the woods and he would hunt toward me. He dropped me off and pointed out where I should stand. He drove away and disappeared. He told me that it would take him thirty to forty minutes to reach me. The place I was standing was on the edge of a small woods but a small band of trees connected with another woods behind me. After twenty to twenty-five minutes I heard a loud commotion in front of me. All of a sudden, several deer were coming right at me and I could see one of them had antlers. Within seconds, these deer ran within a few feet of me. The buck was the last deer and he was nearly on me and he turned away toward his left. I raised my gun and tried to get a bead on the buck. I could not believe how fast all of these deer ran and the buck really took off. Finally, I thought I was lined up with the buck and I shot. Nothing! The buck had disappeared in the next woods. I held my position and waited for Dad and then we would check to see if I had hit the buck. It didn't look like it to me.

Dad arrived and I told him what had happened. He laughed and said he had that happen to him once. We found the bucks track and didn't find any hair or blood. Dad looked to see if he could see where my bullet went. I showed Dad where I thought the buck was when I shot and sure enough we found where my bullet went into the snow, apparently below the buck. I will admit, my heart was racing when I saw the buck.

That evening we skinned the deer and cut it up. Mom canned some of it, several packages were frozen and the rest Dad was going to take to a market that makes sausage, jerky and breakfast sausage.

I wondered if my brother, Sam, had gotten to go hunting with Howard, so I called him. He had gone hunting and Howard shot at a buck but didn't hit it. He said he really enjoyed the day. Carol went to Aunt Joans house. I told Sam I had read about Krag and really enjoyed it. He said it was his favorite story in that book. He also thought Scotty didn't play fair when he sneaked up behind Krag and shot the ram. I told Sam that I thought Scotty had an obsession to shoot the ram. It sounded like he almost didn't shoot but then his old hunter instinct took over and the ram died. Too bad Scotty did not tell the ram, "I could have shot you and I won't chase you anymore. When Scotty shot the ram, he sealed his own fate."

I asked Sam, "If you had been Scotty, would you have shot the ram?" He said, "I have wondered about that very thing and, no, I would not have shot such a noble animal as Krag."

Sam sounded good and said he is getting along alright. He said, "Carol cries some but, day by day, she is getting over Mom not being here. Aunt Joan has really taken good care of Carol."

Late Sunday, November 20, 1948

On Sunday, Dad and I went hunting near my summer campsite. We slowly hunted past the campsite and crossed the little stream. I was close to the Beaver and Dad was closer to the railroad tracks. All at once, I heard a deer running hard going north. A big buck had been lying in some thick brush and I was able to get within about thirty yards before it jumped up. The brush was very thick where the buck was but it was running very fast and I may have been able to shoot but I knew Dad was somewhere on the other side of the deer so I did not shoot. This buck sure looked like the ten-pointer I saw last summer. My heart was really pounding at the sight of this beautiful animal. I did not feel bad that I could not get a shot off.

I headed toward where I thought Dad was and when I found him I told him about the big buck. We talked about me not wanting to shoot this ten-pointer because I felt like I am his friend. Dad said, "I don't like to kill other animals either but I enjoy the challenge of trying to outsmart the animal and I guess as hunters we have been conditioned to try to kill the animals we are hunting for. I sometimes think I could get as much thrill out of hunting if I used a camera instead of a gun." WOW!

We talked some more and decided that we will continue to hunt and try to remember that we are harvesting the bucks and the deer population needs to be kept under control. Dad also said that the deer hunting is an exciting time to be in the woods under all kinds of conditions. He said he has many wonderful memories of deer hunting including today when he was hunting with his son on a beautiful, sunny day.

Monday, November 21, 1948

This morning was windy and snow was falling. We decided to hunt a woods southwest of town. Dad had permission to hunt there and the wind is out of the northwest, which would be fine for us to hunt into the wind. We arrived at the woods, separated and began to slowly hunt towards the northwest. Shortly after I started, I found fresh deer tracks in this brushy woods. I tried to follow these tracks but the brush was so thick I could not follow the tracks. I looked in the direction that the tracks were going. I saw deer feet moving about forty yards away. There were several feet that were slowly moving north. My heart was really beating. I carefully tried to get around the brush and hoped this group of deer would come out where I could see them.

Finally, the deer did emerge and there were five does and fawns. I could see antlers of a buck still in the brush so I slipped the safety off and raised the gun and waited for the buck to step out where I could see it. All at once, I heard a deer snort right behind me. I turned and there was a buck bounding off with big, long bounds. All the other deer, including the buck in the brush, were bounding away from me too. The group in front of me were headed toward where I thought Dad was. I waited for a shot but there was none. I continued slowly hunting toward the northwest. Lots of brush, but I looked for a route that wasn't quite so brushy. By now we had hunted for about two hours when I saw a dark shape on the ground in the heavy brush. I realized that it must be a deer and it was lying down but I could not see any antlers. I was not even sure it was a deer. I slowly took a few steps and now was about fifty yards away from it. I took a few more steps and I still could not see any antlers as the brush was very thick. I did think it was a deer. Now I was about forty yards from this dark shape. All at once, this dark shape jumped up and ran and now I could see it was a buck with a nice rack. I knew Dad was in the woods some place so I did not want to take a chance on shooting. The buck quickly disappeared. My heart was really beating. I stood still and was ready in case the buck is still in the area. Finally, I followed the bucks track and found it circled toward the south and then toward the east. It went behind Dad as he hunted toward the northwest.

I found Dad's tracks and followed them until I could see him. I told him what I had seen and so far Dad had not seen any deer. The last buck would now be downwind of our scent so if he was still in these woods we would have to circle to the south and then go to the east edge of the woods and try to get him.

We followed that plan and slowly started hunting into the wind. All at once, I heard a commotion and saw movement in the brush to the north of me. Finally, I could see it was a buck and was running hard to the east. I raised my gun and tried to get a bead on the buck. Finally, I felt I was on target and pulled the trigger. Nothing happened. I didn't take the safety off!

This didn't look like the buck that was lying down so I thought that buck may still be ahead of me somewhere. I had gone about one hundred fifty yards when I could see a deer standing about ninety yards away. It was looking to the south, maybe toward Dad and it was broadside to me. It was in a brushy place but not as thick as some places. The deer had its head up but suddenly it dropped its head and it was a buck! This was my chance! I took the safety off, raised the rifle and aimed just behind the bucks shoulder. I took a breath, held it and just at that instant the buck walked forward behind a brushy spot. I followed the buck and it presented me with a decent target, so I pulled the trigger. The buck kept on walking but now it angled away from me. I put another cartridge in the chamber but the buck disappeared. I slowly walked to where the buck was when I shot and found no trace of blood or hair. I searched for evidence of where my bullet hit and, there it was, a distance away so I concluded that I shot over the buck. I don't think I had buck fever but maybe that is why my shot missed.

Dad came to see what I had shot at. I explained all that went on and Dad chuckled. "It was a long shot and you are a good shot, but you did what many hunters do by anticipating the recoil of the rifle. You instinctively lift the gun an instant before the gun fires. Don't feel bad, I have had my share of missed shots over the deer."

Tuesday, November 22, 1948

Dad had to work today and I am not allowed to hunt deer unless I am with him. I helped Mom with some things in the house. Last night I called Joe to see how he had done deer hunting and he did not have any luck yet but he has seen several deer but no bucks. I want to write more about *The Mob and the Deer Hunter.*

Ted slept for several hours and finally woke up about noon on Monday. Ann was right by his bed and was very relieved that Ted was awake. Ted had a little trouble recalling what had happened. He had no recollection of the ambulance ride or anything at the hospital. Ted's vital signs were improving but he was still fighting an infection. Ted was groggy and had a difficult time focusing on what Ann was speaking about. Ann encouraged Ted to go back to sleep and in a few minutes he was sound asleep.

Ann asked to be taken home so she could see Jake and Lois and maybe bring them to the hospital if it is allowed. The deputy on duty called the sheriff to see if another deputy could take Ann home. In a few minutes a deputy was on the way and Ann was taken home and a very happy reunion was held.

Ann checked with Christ Olson to see how the milking and chores were going. He replied, "Everything is A-OK. Tell Ted not to worry, just get well." Ann had Jake and Lois get into the car and they headed to the hospital.

When Ann and the kids arrived at the hospital, Jake and Lois looked at Ted and looked at Ann with a worried look on their faces. Jake said, "Dad looks bad." Ann told the kids, "Your dad needs to sleep but he is getting better." Lois began to cry and that woke Ted up. At first he had a difficult time comprehending what was going on but then he realized that Jake and Lois were in the room. In a little while, he called the kids to his bedside and wanted to hug his children. Ann helped both kids up on Ted's bed so they could hug each other. Ted appeared to be feeling better. Ann thought he looked the best he had since coming to the hospital.

Later that day, a doctor came in to check on Ted and was amazed at how much progress Ted had made. His vital signs were nearly normal and his wounds looked like they should this soon after being admitted. Ann was very happy to see that Ted seemed to be like the Ted she had loved for many years.

Jake had many questions to ask Ted but most of them were about what he saw in the woods, like birds, bunnies and deer. Lois wanted to tell her dad about her dolls and how worried they were that he had been hurt. Ted listened carefully and tentatively and was very happy to have them ask questions and tell him things. Later that day he told Ann, "There were several times during the ordeal I really thought that I would never see my family again."

Ann got the kids settled for a few minutes and told Ted what the sheriff had told her about the car being hit by a train and the two occupants were killed. She said, "The state portable crime lab staff were examining all six bodies to identify each one. The FBI and Illinois Attorney General are also involved. Hopefully, we will know more about these men and the two black Cadillac's. The sheriff and all the deputies have been wonderful. One of the deputies was wounded and was in a room just down the hall but he recovered enough so he went home yesterday."

By early evening, Ann gathered up the children and they all told Ted good night and they left the hospital and went home. Ann was very relieved at Ted's progress but still worried if someone might try to silence Ted either at the hospital or later at their home. The other issue troubling

Ann was, how are we going to pay for the hospital bill? She knew their farm was a wonderful place to live and raise the kids, but there was never enough money to do much more than purchase the necessities. She really had no idea how much the hospital charges might be and it was worrisome to her.

Late Tuesday, November 22, 1948

I have thought about shooting at the buck yesterday, many times. For one thing, the sight of a buck is very exciting. They truly are a spectacular animal. Maybe I really don't want to shoot a buck. I certainly thought I was trying to shoot the bucks, but I missed. I can picture those bucks and the other five bucks I have seen in the first three days of deer season.

Sitting in my room and writing this diary I thought about each of the five bucks that I didn't get a shot at. I could picture each buck and what the situation was of each. Was I alert enough? Should I have shot quicker?

I have seen seven bucks and only got two shots off and I have not shot a buck. Maybe I am a poor hunter. I am almost afraid to try hunting again for fear I may fail again. Dad has to work until noon tomorrow and we are planning to go deer hunting when he gets home. I need to talk to Dad to see if he ever had doubts like I have now. I called Jim and he and his dad each shot a buck. They have been busy skinning deer and cutting up the meat. Jed missed a buck today and was kicking himself because the buck came up behind him and when Jed heard it, he turned around and the buck saw him. It bounded away and Jed got three shots off but all missed. He said he really got excited when he saw the buck. It had a real nice rack.

Late Wednesday, November 23, 1948

Dad got home at noon and I was ready. We decided to go back to the woods where I shot at the second buck. It was a clear day but very cold, below zero when we left home. We decided to follow the same plan as we did when we hunted two days ago. The slight breeze was out of the northwest. After a few steps in the woods, I realized that the snow was 'crunchy' and it was very difficult to walk without making noise. However, any deer walking anywhere near me would also make noise that I could hear.

I carefully followed my same route and uncovered my ears so I could hear any deer movement. I approached the thick brush where I first saw the group of deer. I carefully looked but did not see any deer. I began to move

to my right to continue moving into the breeze. I stopped when I heard something moving to my left. It was a squirrel. A few more steps and more sounds of something moving from my left. Another squirrel? - NOT. About eighty yards away, a group of deer were heading toward the northwest running but not flat out. I counted five with no antlers and was disappointed, but then I saw another deer following the group. This one had antlers - nice ones. I knew Dad was somewhere to my left and I could not shoot at this buck until he got west of me. The buck continued running to the northwest and by the time I could safely shoot, it was over one-hundred yards away and getting farther all the time. Finally, it stopped about one hundred yards away and offered no target whatsoever. I carefully began walking toward the buck but going more to my right than straight at it. Because of the distance and the slight breeze in my favor, I thought I might get in position to get off a long shot. There were lots of trees which helped hide me from the view of the deer. Finally, I was within about ninety yards and had a possible shot from behind the right side of the buck. I put my rifle up and took the safety off. I took a bead on where I thought the heart was but, all at once, the buck started running toward the north. I followed him with my rifle and he came into a small open area so I took a shot. The buck kept running like it had not been hit. I could not get another shot off and the buck ran out of sight.

Boy, I was nervous. I reloaded the rifle and went to where the deer was when I shot. I found a glob of dark hair but no blood. I followed the track for over one- hundred yards and still no blood. About then Dad showed up and I explained where I was and we went back to the glob of hair. Dad looked at it carefully and said it looked like hair from the bucks back. He thought I must have been a little high with my shot. We went back to where I was standing when I shot. Dad said, "It was a long shot, over one-hundred yards and the buck was running. I may have missed it too, so don't feel bad."

Thursday, November 24, 1948

It is Thanksgiving Day and Dad has the day off. It is snowing hard and the wind is blowing. We decided to hunt until noon and Dad had a spot in mind east of town. We arrived at the woods and stayed together instead of hunting away from each other. Dad dug two portable stools out of the car trunk and said we will find a good looking spot to sit and let the deer come to us. About two-hundred yards into the woods we came to a small hill in a grove of oak trees. We sat about four feet apart. I looked south and Dad looked to the north. Dad said that this way we can sit and quietly visit in whispers and keep looking for deer.

The wind was out of the west and visibility was poor. We kept our hands over the actions of our rifles to prevent getting moisture in around the bolt. Dad said that he and his dad hunted this way a few times. In fact, they were sitting very close to this very spot about fifteen years ago when a large nine-point buck came from the west. Dad continued, "My dad saw it approach and told me to slowly turn around and shoot this big buck. It was walking with its head down and when it got about seventy yards away, I took a shot at it. The buck kept walking with its head down. By now it was about fifty-five yards away. I fired again and this time the buck dropped in its tracks and it was a beauty, seventeen and one-half inch spread."

Dad and I had been sitting together for about one and one-half hours when Dad said he saw a deer coming this way. He told me to turn around and watch the deer to see if it is a buck. The deer was over one-hundred yards away and was moving from southwest toward the northeast. Enough snow had fallen on the brush so it was difficult to see if it was a buck. Finally, we could see antlers but before I could get a bead on it the buck disappeared behind some snowy branches. Apparently it stopped behind the brush and we watched for at least ten minutes and still no buck. Dad thought it may have laid down or went straight away, keeping the snowy brush between it and us. Dad told me he would make a wide circle and come toward me but also in line with where we thought the buck might be. He said it would take at least thirty minutes, so stay alert.

A few minutes after Dad left, I heard some noise behind me so I turned around very slowly. About forty yards from me stood a doe with two fawns. Her head was held high and after about five seconds she raised her right front leg and stamped the ground with a hard move. All three deer had me in their sights and after about another ten seconds the doe gave a short snort and all three whirled around and left with high bounds, their white tails very visible.

I returned to watching the spot where we last saw the buck. Finally, I could see Dad approaching and he came right to where I was sitting. "The buck turned and went away from us and our view was blocked by the snow clad brush," he said.

We sat for another hour and both of us were wet from snow melting on us. We decided to head for home. Our rifles will need to be taken apart, dried off and oiled. Dad told about a time when he had a different bolt action rifle and on a day like this he trailed deer through thick brush for several hours. When he got home he wiped the rifle and bolt good and then oiled the rifle and the bolt. The next day was about 10° F. below zero when he got to the woods. By late afternoon he saw a buck and raised his rifle and took a shot at it. Nothing happened! He ejected that shell and tried another one. He got the same result. He headed for home and once there he took the bolt out and examined it to see how to get it apart. He thought water had got in around the firing pin and frozen. He found out how to take the bolt apart and sure enough, the firing pin had a couple drops of water on it. The very cold weather that day froze the water into ice so Dad had hunted with a rifle that would not shoot for most of the day. We both took our rifle bolts apart to check for water and to oil them.

Mom and Dad had invited our neighbors, Mr. and Mrs. Mast for Thanksgiving dinner this evening. Mr. Mast is a retired railroad engineer and both of them are very nice people. Dad carved the turkey and Mom asked me to mash the potatoes. The meal was wonderful and talk during the meal was about the coal strike by John L. Lewis and most of the coal miners. Both homes had some coal but not enough to get through the winter. Everyone is hoping for an end to the strike.

Sunday, November 27, 1948

Dad had to work both Friday and Saturday. Friday I spent four hours at the gym shooting baskets and playing a few make-up games. Joe and Jim were both there but Jed was hunting with some cousins from Eau Claire. Saturday we had a blizzard. There was a lot of snow and big drifts were developing. I decided to try to finish my story, *The Mob and the Deer Hunter.*

Ted was able to leave the hospital Wednesday afternoon. A deputy sat outside his door at the hospital all the time he was there. He was very happy to get home. His face looked fine except for the stitches above his left eye. The bullet wound in his left shoulder was healing well but the dressing on the exit wound needed changing each day for a few days. Ann could do that. Jake and Lois were very happy that their dad was back home. They thought that a bad man had shot their dad and might be coming after him to shoot him again. They did not know about any dead men or that they were mobsters. Ted and Ann will tell them more in a few days, but for now what they know is good enough.

Christ Olson continued milking and doing chores but Ted did go out to be with Christ on Thanksgiving Day. He still was weak so he didn't stay out very long. A deputy was still on duty and sat in his car all the time, 24 hours a day.

About 1:00 p.m. Christ and his wife, Evelyn, drove in with Thanksgiving dinner for Ted, Ann, Jake and Lois. A big platter of turkey, dressing, mashed potatoes, gravy, rolls, relishes and a pumpkin pie. Evelyn had talked to Ann about doing this for them since Ann had been so busy and it was very much appreciated and very good. Everyone did a good job of stuffing themselves. Ted also invited the deputy in to eat with them and he gratefully accepted. Jake and Lois were a little intimidated by the deputy with his uniform on, the radio, sidearm and in general he looked imposing to them.

Deer season ended and Ted was able to return to doing the milking and other chores. He was tired and needed to rest during the day but he was getting stronger by the day. Wednesday, midmorning, the sheriff drove into the yard. He spoke to the deputy and the deputy drove away. The sheriff and another man came to the door and asked Ann if they could come in. The other man was an FBI agent from Chicago.

They all sat around the kitchen table and Ann asked Jake and Lois to play in the living room for awhile. The FBI agent said, "Between the States of Wisconsin and Illinois crime labs, all of the dead men have been identified. All were very well known to the FBI and Chicago and Illinois police departments. They all had rewards for their capture or death and all have served time in federal prisons. They have been charged with extortion, embezzlement, income tax evasion and fraud."

"The two men that Ted shot, the 'Bullhead' and the 'Zipper' have a reward of $2,000 on each of them. We examined the bullets found in each man and found they came from Ted's rifle. Therefore, Ted is entitled to the cash totaling $4,000." Ted and Ann were shocked. "All six dead men were members of the same mob and the boss 'Chicago

Joe' was killed in the wreck with the train. The man you saw shot apparently had double-crossed 'Chicago Joe' and he had to go," the FBI agent said.

"These men were staying in a cabin near Stone Lake, not far from where their car was hit by a train. Our sources think that this gang only had six members and now they are all dead." He said, "Also, your names will not show up in any of the reports by the crime labs or the FBI. One more thing. Since Ted was injured during attacks by these mobsters, I have been authorized to give you, Ted and Ann, an additional $2,000 in cash. Here it is." Ann nearly fell off her chair and Ted could not believe it. "The FBI has ordered a gag order on all media as far as not telling your names, where you live or any other information that may identify you," he said.

The sheriff and the FBI agent left and Ann gave Ted a big hug and said, "One very large worry I had was how were we going to pay for the hospital bill. I hope this money will cover it." THE END

Monday, November 28, 1948

Deer season is over for this year. Sunday morning the storm was over. The work sure wasn't as Dad had to shovel on High Street to get home from work Sunday morning. The snow was so deep that the locomotives could not get through it south of Spooner. A plow on an engine had to be sent to open the rails. Dad was ten hours late getting home. We had five foot deep drifts by our house and right in front of the garage. Sunday morning, I shoveled the driveway up toward the garage. By the time I got there the drift was almost as tall as I was and I really didn't know where to shovel the snow. I had shoveled for two hours when Dad came home. Between the two of us we got a path opened so Dad could drive the car into the garage. Our neighbors were all busy shoveling their drifts, too.

Out of town, some roads were blocked. Eventually the heavy equipment began to break through the drifts. The county has several all-wheel drive Oshkosh giant trucks with

V-plows on them. These trucks are loaded with salted sand and are very powerful, but apparently many drifts required several runs at them in order to break through. The City of Spooner had two graders with V-plows and the drivers were doing their best, but this storm was about the biggest that anyone could remember. People reported up to thirty inches in the woods where it had not drifted.

Our rifles were all cleaned and oiled so on Sunday night we could put them away. My season was exciting even though I didn't get a buck. I saw several bucks and many does and fawns. I have a healthy respect for the deer, they are very alert, fast runners and difficult to shoot, at least for me. Now they face a much more dangerous foe than hunters. Deep snow is one of the worst enemies in this area. Deer are browsers which means they bite off the tips of brush, branches, blackberry bushes and other shoots that reach above the snow. Acorns are sought after but once the snow gets deep the deer can't find them. Dad thinks that this storm, with its deep snow, will put many deer into yards and many will die of starvation. One thing I learned in my forestry class is that deer have hollow hair which protects them from bitter cold weather. I really respect the deer for its ability to survive and thrive under extreme conditions.

It's Monday and it is the first day back to school after deer season. There are lots of stories about big bucks, little bucks, misses and other stories about the big hunt. Many rural roads are impassable so attendance is down to about half today. One thing that bothered me was hearing kids talk about shooting does and fawns since this was a bucks only season. For whatever reason, I could not possibly knowingly break the law. Dad would be very upset because he knows we all have to follow the laws. He has told me that he knows some families really need the meat and some even poach deer in the off season. He would not turn them in but he would not break the law. Dad also really harped to me to be sure it is a legal buck before you shoot. Also, know what is behind whatever you are shooting at. Rifle bullets can glance off objects and go two or three miles.

Dad is a very safe hunter and reads the rule book carefully. He makes me read it too, and I know he would not break any of the game laws or fishing laws. Dad knows a great deal about hunting and fishing and I hope to follow in his footsteps.

Basketball practice was at 7:00 p.m. this week and Coach Jones really made us work. Man to man defense, blocking out when rebounding, wind sprints and free throws. We play Rice Lake this Thursday and they are really strong. There are two kids taller than any of our team so we really worked on rebounding and blocking shots. This late practice is hard on families. When do we eat supper? You can't go to a hard practice after eating a big meal. Most of us have a small snack and eat supper when we get home about 9:00 p.m. Beside meals, getting a ride home can be difficult as none of us can drive yet. Lots of town kids invite team members to their house to eat a snack and do homework. Schools gets out at 3:30 p.m. and this a long time until 7:00 p.m. We seem to be making it work.

Friday, December 2, 1948

There was a big game with Rice Lake last night. It was Spooner freshmen 27, Rice Lake freshmen 26. Wow! That was a hard fought game. We out-rebounded them twenty-three rebounds to seventeen. Coach Jones was really excited! I scored five points and made three out of four free throws. Joe had nine points and twelve rebounds. I had six rebounds. I really like to play defense and rebound. Darrell had six points.

On Thursday I got a letter from Savannah. She is in the varsity band and last week there was competition for first chair in the third section of clarinets and she won. I could tell by her letter that she was really proud of this accomplishment. She said that from time to time other members of the third section can challenge her by requesting a competition. She said she has to practice daily.

Savannah said her family is planning to come to the

cabin the day after Christmas. They would stay through Friday, December 30th. They know that there has been a blizzard and maybe the road to the cabin will not be plowed. Then again it may get warm and the snow will melt. We, Mom, Dad and me, are inviting you and your mom and dad to come to the cabin and do winter things like ice fish, go snowshoeing, or sit by the fireplace and play games or just visit. You would be welcome to stay overnight, if you can. If you have a sleeping bag, you should bring it.

Sunday, December 4, 1958

Yesterday, Joe asked me if I wanted to go ice fishing with him and his dad. I said I would like to and asked what they were going to fish for. "Big northern on Dilly Lake. We will pick you up at 9:00 a.m.". "What do I need for tackle," I asked. "We have enough for you. See you in a little bit."

By 9:00 a.m. Joe and his dad picked me up. They had already stopped at the sport shop and had picked up minnows, about five to six inches long. We drove to Dilly Lake which is northeast of town about eight to ten miles. We parked the car and headed toward the lake. We came to some tag alders and Joe's dad took a hatchet and cut several branches off the alders and we took them out on the lake. I didn't say anything, but I sure wondered how we would use them. Joe carried a bucket, an ice chisel and a dipper with holes in it. I had the minnow pail.

We went to a spot on the southeast part of the lake. Finally, we stopped and Joe started making a hole in the ice with the ice chisel. The ice was only about eight to ten inches thick and it didn't take long for Joe to make a hole, about twelve inches in diameter. Next, he chipped into the ice about two feet from the hole. Joe's dad brought one of the larger branches over and put the big end in the small hole beside the larger hole. Now Joe took out the dipper and started dipping the ice chips out of the big hole. He put these chips around the base of the branch which was leaning over the big hole. Joe splashed water on the ice chips and before long it was firmly planted in the ice.

Joe's dad dug into the bucket and brought out some thick, green, heavy fish line that was wrapped around a wire frame about four inches by four inches. There was a treble hook on one end and on the other end Joe's dad tied a smaller alder branch. He reached into the bucket and caught a minnow and hooked it through the back below the fin. He then dropped the minnow through the big hole and let it hang about three feet below the surface. He then carried the small branch out a short distance until the line was taut. He then came back to the hole and put the line over one of the branches of the alder, positioned over the hole. Now the set up was complete.

By now I could see how this was all going to work. A northern pike grabs the minnow and the bush above the hole vibrates to alert me. The fish may run off a distance before it swallows the minnow and the treble hook. This action will cause the smaller branch to move over the snow and hopefully I could reach the branch to set the hook and catch the northern pike.

While I watched Joe's dad, Joe had made another hole and had rigged up a branch over it. I helped Joe's dad and we baited the hook and got the line set up like the first hole. In a few minutes, we had the third line all baited and set up like the others. Now we stood and watched the bushes above the hole. The minnow could make the branch wiggle a little.

After a few minutes, one of the bushes gave a violent jerk and the small branch started moving toward the hole. Joe's dad ran to it and got a hold of the line and set the hook. Immediately there was a strong pull on the line and Joe's dad began to pull the line in. Presently Joe ran to the hole with a small gaff hook and reached down in the hole to the fish and lifted it out. Wow! It must have weighed at least ten pounds. Next he used a tool that spread the northern pikes mouth open and now Joe could reach in with a needle-nose pliers and remove the hook. I was impressed.

Throughout the remainder of the day we caught nine northern pike. The biggest was at least fifteen pounds. The smallest was about three pounds. Several of them were in the seven to ten pound range. Finally we called it a day and pulled up the lines, put the northern pike on a stringer and headed for home. It was decided that I would take one small one and two of the seven to ten pound pike. I protested and would only take one of the ten pounders. Finally they agreed and on the way home they explained how I should fillet these fish. I took care of cleaning and filleting the fish when I got home. Mom showed me what size package I should make. We put several packages in the freezer but Mom kept out a good sized fillet to have for supper. It was good the way Mom prepared it.

Sunday afternoon I listened to the Green Bay Packers playing the New York Giants in Green Bay. The game ended in a 10 to 10 tie. After the game I wanted to write something that I have been thinking about since this summer. I really enjoy watching running water, maybe everyone does. The water in Beaver Brook was in motion most of the time but there were pools where the water seemed to stand still. What the heck is water anyway? It can be in any size body from oceans to lakes to rivers to rain drops. I have learned about water molecules and I know they are attracted to each other and this creates surface tension that allows little insects called 'water striders' to run around on top of the water. This is the reason water can creep up a small glass tube or a little distance up a water glass.

Water can evaporate and leave any mud or other impurities behind. The clouds are water vapor and when conditions are right it rains or snows out of these clouds. If there is a large amount of rain or snow melt, it will run off into a stream, river, lake, marsh or swamp. Apparently the water can be used over and over forever but for a period of time it may be what makes Beaver Brook.

Dad said the Beaver begins in a spring fed lake south of County Road B, named Lutz Lake. Within a quarter of a mile, just after flowing under County Road B, more water is added to the Beaver from an artesian well. This is a well that the water flows out of all by itself. Downstream a short distance is a small reservoir and then a larger one.

The Beaver continues flowing northwest and many small springs add their water to the Beaver. The Beaver grows larger as it flows northwest and a fair size stream flows under the trestle and into the Beaver. Farther downstream the water from the beaver pond joins the brook. This is a large flow of water and the Beaver is noticeably larger. More spring water is added until it joins the Yellow River after flowing four and one-half miles. By now the Beaver is twenty to twenty-five feet wide in many places but it is still flowing.

I am like that brook. I started out small and added size as I got older. These little springs are like my development, both physically and mentally. When I think of how much my knowledge level has grown in my fifteen years I am impressed. I have learned to do many, many physical things like throw and hit a baseball, catch the baseball, and shoot a basketball. I can throw and catch a football, run with the football and shift the ball from one hand to another.

I have learned to catch many different fish. I can hunt partridge and squirrel. I have learned to shoot my deer rifle. I learned how to tie my shoes, dress myself, brush my teeth and take care of my body. I learned how to say words and then put them into sentences. I have learned how to count and what the alphabet is and how to use it. I learned to tell time, count money, write words and sentences as well as sing songs.

I have learned about the constitution of our country, how a democracy works, and why Americans have been involved in several wars to preserve our democracy. I have learned to have a great respect for our veterans and their sacrifice to preserve our freedom. I need to do more thinking about this flowing brook.

Friday, December 9, 1948

Spooner freshmen basketball 24, Cumberland freshmen 19. We played good defense and out rebounded them twenty-one to eleven. Coach Jones was very pleased. We hit five out of six free throws. Joe is our best scorer and rebounder. Darrell had seven points. I didn't play in the second half. Coach Jones said he wanted to give Tom a chance and he did well. I better try harder. I don't like sitting on the bench. Snow has been melting as the weather is very warm for December. The length of daylight is nearly at the bottom of the well. That is alright with me as I really don't like wintertime darkness.

Saturday, December 10, 1948

Dad didn't have to work today and asked me to go with him while he went out to see one of the men he works with. He lives about five miles north of town. We drove in and Dad went to the door and his friend came out. They talked and in a few minutes Dad came to the car and told me to come with him. I went with Dad to a shed with a sliding door which Dad slid open. There sat a car, covered with a tarp. Dad pulled the tarp off and there it was. THE OLD 1937 FORD!! It was our old car that I thought Dad had traded in on the new 1949 Ford. He said, "The car wasn't worth much as a trade-in so we decided to keep it so maybe you could drive it to go hunting, fishing or visiting Joe or the other kids." I could hardly believe it.

Dad said, "You will be sixteen this coming July 20th and will be eligible to get a drivers license, if you can pass a driving test. On January 20th you will be fifteen and one-half years old and you can apply for a learners permit. This allows you a chance to learn to drive but only if either your mom or I are with you. After you get your license you can not drive it to school and you can not have more than one person with you unless your mom and I are with you. After you are seventeen, you are on your own to drive as you see fit.

I could hardly believe it. I would have the '37 Ford to drive. I really like that car. I know Dad will show me how to change the oil, grease it, take care of the air filters and do whatever maintenance is needed, such as changing spark plugs and points. That will be a lot of responsibility, but it is exciting.

On the way back home, Dad stopped at the police station and we went in and Dad asked for a copy of the Wisconsin Highway Laws of Driving. He also asked for a learners driving permit application. I had heard other classmates talk about getting their drivers license and I was interested but I really thought getting to be sixteen was a long way off. I must be a day dreamer. I spent the rest of the day studying the driving laws and they seemed complicated.

Friday, December 16, 1948

Hayward freshmen basketball 35, Spooner freshmen 25. We got out scored, out rebounded, out everything. We stunk the place up! Their team hit nearly every shot they took. They had two big kids that really scored and grabbed nearly every rebound. Joe was no match for both of them. I did not start but I played all of the second half and my play was lousy. Three free throws and I missed them all. Coach Jones did not have much to say after the game. He did say that we would be ready for these guys when we play them in February.

Wednesday, December 21, 1948

This is the last day of school before Christmas vacation and everyone is happy. In forestry class, we had a little party and Mr. Peterson furnished cake and ice cream. We had a little contest between four teams picked by Mr. Peterson. He asked questions about trees and forestry. The captain of each team had a white rubber balloon on a string and we sat in a semi-circle around Mr. Peterson. When the captain thought his or her team had the correct answer the captain gently threw his balloon on the floor. If it was the first balloon they gave the answer and if it was correct that team got twenty-five points. If it was wrong, the team lost fifty points and the next fastest team could try to answer. It was a lot of fun. The team I was on was second with seventy-five points. We lost fifty points on a wrong answer and we had been in the lead at that point. Merry Christmas.

We didn't have basketball practice after school so I went downtown by myself. I had seen a nifty bracelet in the jewelry store window. If it was still there, I wanted to buy it for Savannah. I had $17.00 and hoped that would be enough. I had never bought a gift for a girl before and I was nervous.

As I approached the store, I looked ahead of me and here came 'Rough' and 'Tough'. I walked past the jewelry store and met those guys and, of course, they wanted to know where I was going. I told them I was going to see my dad at the depot. 'Rough' wanted to know if my dad would take them up into an engine. I said, "I don't think that is allowed." 'Tough' said, "Why don't we ask him and then we will know." We went to the depot and looked for my dad and, of course, we did not find him. We decided to walk home. Once I ditched those guys I hightailed it back to the jewelry store. The bracelet was several copper scenes fastened with little copper rings. I liked it and hoped Savannah would like it too. I finally asked the price and it was $15.95. I paid for it and asked if it could be gift wrapped. The clerk wrapped it for me and I headed home.

Late Thursday, December 22, 1948

The principal, Mr. Gold, announced on Wednesday that he had a list of elderly people who need someone to shovel their driveways and sidewalks. Anyone wanting to do this must do this gratis. If someone offers to pay, you could take the money and donate it to the Salvation Army here in Spooner. Stop and get a list of addresses of people who need shoveling. We have several in the country, too.

Joe, 'Rough', 'Tough' and I picked up twelve addresses in our part of town. We met at 8:30 a.m. for our first 'dig-out'. It didn't take the four of us long to shovel the folks out. A lady came out and thanked us and gave us each a quarter. We thanked her and went on to the next address. By noon we had done ten of the addresses and had collected $10.50. One home seemed empty but we shoveled it anyway. We went to my house and had some lunch. We went back to finish the other two addresses which did not take very long. We collected $2.00. We saw two houses that hadn't been shoveled and Joe went to the door and asked if we could shovel their driveway and sidewalks at no cost. The people were thrilled and when we were finished they donated fifty cents to each of us and a couple chocolate chip cookies apiece. The next home was almost a copy of the last one and we each got fifty cents plus a couple oatmeal cookies with raisins. We put all our money in a small bag and it totaled $16.40. I said I had $1.05 to contribute. 'Rough' had eighty cents, 'Tough' had ninety-five cents and Joe had fifty-five cents. We now had a total of $19.75.

We wanted to get at least $20.00. 'Tough' said, "Let's see if Mr. Gold wants his place shoveled. It is only one and one-half blocks away." 'Tough' knocks on the door and Mrs. Gold answered. 'Tough' explained what we were doing and said, "We want to get $20.00 and we will finish digging out your driveway and walk for twenty-five cents." "My, my, that is a generous offer and I will be happy to oblige you." We made this snow fly and we were just finishing when Mr. Gold drove in to his freshly shoveled driveway. Mrs. Gold came out and told Mr. Gold about our offer. Mr. Gold said, "Wonderful, but we will pay more than that. How about $1.25?" Mrs. Gold said, "I already had $2.25 ready to pay these wonderful boys". Mr. Gold said, "Fine, we will give them $3.50 and here is sixty cents so you can stop at the Dairy Bar and get a soda." We thanked the Gold's and then 'Tough' said, "Why don't we give our collection to Mr. Gold now?" We agreed and so did Mr. Gold, so we handed our sack with $23.25 in it to Mr. Gold He was amazed that we had raised that much.

Friday, December 23, 1948

It is a snowy day so other than shoveling snow I am going to read the rest the book, *Wild Animals I Have Known*. The last story in the book is about Lobo, a huge wolf that lived in Texas. Lobo was the leader of a wolf pack that were killing cattle on a large ranch there. The pack was well known to the ranchers and the cowboys that worked there. Attempts to trap or shoot these wolves were successful once in a while. The author was hired to dispatch this wolf pack and he carefully studied their activities. He eventually caught all the lesser members of the pack so only Lobo and his white mate, Blancka, remained. Finally Blancka was trapped and killed. Lobo followed the scent to the ranch and was so enraged that he killed two of the ranchers dogs. His deep powerful howl could be heard by everyone at the ranch and it sent shivers of fear through those that heard it.

The author took all of Blanckas feet and gently made her tracks over each of four buried powerful traps. The body was dragged to where the traps were buried and then picked up. The next day cattle could be heard making a big fuss and upon investigation, the powerful wolf, Lobo, was caught with each of his feet in a trap. The cattle came to torment their old nemesis and had come in very close, realizing that the wolf could not hurt them. The author had a carbine rifle and held it near the wolfs head. The wolf snapped at the end of the barrel and left a mark on it. Wow! Lobo was subdued and taken back to the ranch alive. The pack horse didn't like the wolf on its back but they got Lobo to the ranch where he was put in a secured enclosure and given water and food, which he refused. Once he let out a powerful howl, apparently to his pack to come to his aid. There was no pack. The word spread that Lobo had been captured and people came to see this legendary wolf. Lobo laid with his head up and didn't acknowledge anyone. Though apparently unhurt, Lobo was dead in the morning. Some say he died of a broken heart.

There are wolves around here. I heard them howl last summer and at least one walked very near my tent. Apparently, Lobo must have been a huge wolf. There are very few wolves in Wisconsin and there is talk about putting them on an endangered list. They are scary.

In the afternoon, I called brother Sam to visit with him. He seemed to be adjusting and he said Carol was doing alright, too. We talked about Lobo and Sam thought it was a very good story. He was sorry that Lobo died at the end of the story but he said he was killing cattle so a price was put on his head. I said, "What if Lobo had lived a thousand years ago, long before there were ranchers and cattle?" Sam said, "Lobo would not have had men coming after him and maybe he would have lived much longer. His pack might have had to defend their territory from other wolf packs. Maybe Lobo might have had to fight an even larger, more powerful wolf and may have been killed, but not by man."

Christmas Eve Day, Saturday, December 24, 1948

It was a busy day. Dad didn't have to work. We put up the Christmas tree and decorated it in the morning. Some of the decorations are from many years ago and were on Dad's grandfather and grandmothers trees. They were beautiful glass balls, shaped like a bunch of grapes. This tree was a balsam fir and I showed Mom how to pop the little blisters on the trunk to get a small flow of balsam oil which is used in oil immersion microscopes. We learned that in my favorite class, forestry.

Mom is busy all afternoon cooking, baking and directing Dad and me about table preparations, chairs and helping in the kitchen - when needed. Otherwise, we needed to stay clear of that room. By early evening, Mom's sister, Rebecca, her husband, Walter, and kids, Jason age fourteen, Beth age twelve and Josh age eight arrived from Minnesota. They are nice folks and I get along with them just fine. Sometimes the kids can act a little snooty, but we manage. They did seem very interested in hearing about my summer camping and fishing. Jason said, "I would really like to camp out like you did. It must have been scary at night." I told him, "It was scary, but I felt safe in my tent."

The four of us played a card game called 'hearts' and Beth was the big winner of the first game. Josh won the second game and I was leading when Dad announced that dinner was on the table. Besides ham, sweet potatoes, cranberries, rolls, pickles and olives, our family has a cabbage roll called halupchi which Mom and Dad made yesterday. It has sauerkraut, sausage, potatoes, rice and onions all ground up and rolled up in a cabbage leaf. While it is cooking, the entire house smells to high heaven, but it tastes good and all of us at the table really like it and we 'pig out'.

All these folks are going to spend the night so I get kicked out of my bed and all of us kids will sleep on the living room floor with lots of blankets. I heard the grownups talking that this will be the last night that anyone stays over because we went to their place last year. Instead, we will alternate but it will be a noon meal so the traveling party can get home. This took an hour to write up. Good night.

Christmas Day, December 25, 1948

Everyone got up early and we all exchanged gifts. I bought Mom a pretty neck scarf and for Dad I got a subscription to *Popular Mechanics*. I got a pair of converse hip boots, as my old ones were too small. I will see if brother Sam can wear them and if so, they are his. I have really admired these converse hip boots. I am really impressed.

Rebecca, Walter and the cousins leave after breakfast as Walters brother and family will come to their home for supper. The same at our house. Dad's brother, Ernest, his wife, Margaret and the kids, Larry age sixteen, Jack age twelve and Sue age ten will arrive from Eau Claire by mid-afternoon. Larry makes me nervous. He is a scruffy looking guy with longer, scraggly hair. He is lean and has a deceptive look about him. I think he smokes because he is always eating sen-sen which has a very strong odor.

Jack, on the other hand, seems like a friendly, likeable boy. He is curious and seems to care about himself and how he interacts with others, like me. Sue is really into music and sits by the radio listening to music a lot. Otherwise she seems nice. My friends and I would probably call Larry a sleeze-ball and would stay away from him. Larry and Sue had no interest in any game, so Jack and I played Black Jack. He was ahead when we stopped to eat supper. It was nearly a re-run of last nights meal, but only Walter and Sue like the halupchi. I noticed that everyone got plenty to eat, even the sleeze-ball.

We had just finished eating and the phone rang. It was for me. It was Earl, my injured marine friend that shared my campsite with me. He said, "I was thinking about you and just wanted to hear your voice and thank you for being my friend and helping at a time when I really needed help." I told him about the big trout that Dad and I caught and put in the Beaver. I also told him about football and basketball and seeing the Packers play the Rams.

Earl said, "My leg is about as good now as it is going to get." He said he does therapy everyday for forty minutes and that has really helped. School is going good but the classes are hard and his study skills are rusty but he will have all B's the first semester. Margaret is doing just fine. He told me that they get along very well and she has been helping him get his study skills back.

I told Earl, "Mom, Dad and I are going to visit Savannah and her parents at the cabin one day this coming week." I told Earl about the last visit to the cabin and how scared we all were when we heard the noise upstairs in the old house. We said goodbye and after I put the phone down, I realized how much I missed Earl. Our time together last summer meant a great deal to both of us. I think we will always be friends.

Monday, December 26, 1948

About noon, Savannah called and told me that everything was plowed out at the cabin. I told Savannah that Dad had to work today and tomorrow and Mom and Dad have already said we could go any day Wednesday to Friday. I asked Mom which day is best. She said, "Let's go Wednesday." I told Savannah about that and she was happy that we could come then.

Today it is snowing. All of my buddies are visiting grandparents out of town. I have thought about trying to write a book for kids. I want to write about a fox family, a saw-whet owl family and a deer and two fawns. The book would be called *'Wild Animal Babies'*.

Fox

It is April in northern Wisconsin. Earlier in the year, a pair of foxes mated and now the mother was about to give birth to her pups, called kits. The two foxes already had prepared a home for the babies. It is in a den, several feet in the ground. The opening for the den faces the south and is in the side of a hill. A large white pine is nearby and roots had to be dug around, but protects the den from other diggers.

The den burrow slopes gently downward and ends in an enlarged, rounded part of the burrow. The foxes gathered soft, dry grass and made a soft bed of dry grass at the end of the burrow. The temperature in the den is well above freezing. It is not warm but it is a snug safe place for baby foxes to be born. Also, it is pitch dark so sense of feel, smell and touch are how the kits, mother and father fox operate in the den.

Finally, the big day arrives and the mother fox, called a vixen, can tell she is about to give birth. This would be her second litter as she had four kits born about this time last year, only one is still alive and lives about five miles away. One kit died after two weeks and another was caught by a trapper in early winter. The third kit was shot by a hunter for the bounty. The mother fox knew the signs when the babies are going to be born.

Deep in the den, the mother fox gave birth to the first kit. The pup arrived on the soft, dry grass and immediately the mother fox began licking the newborn fox. It made tiny high-pitched squeaks but as the mother fox licked her baby, she directed it to one of her nipples, where an ample supply of warm, rich milk awaited the hungry mouth of the baby fox.

In a short time, another baby fox was born and the mother fox gave it the same treatment. This baby was very shy and did not make any tiny, high-pitched squeals. Maybe its name should be 'Shy'. Being shy didn't prevent 'Shy' from getting licked off by its mother and then it found a nipple to nurse on and get plenty of warm, rich milk.

About twenty minutes later, a third baby fox was born on the dry grass of the den. It was smaller and slimmer. This baby was very active and immediately crawled away from its mother. Mother fox gently picked the baby up with her mouth and put it down where she could lick it. This action caused the baby to settle down and it too began to seek a nipple and suckle its mothers warm, rich milk. Once it found its nipple, it drank its fill and then fell asleep.

The baby fox is born with its eyes closed and in a few days the eyes open to reveal blue-gray eyes. Their fur is gray and they have a white tip on the end of their tail. They have short legs and their body is short and stubby. When they are full grown they will have larger legs, a longer, slimmer body and they will have beautiful red fur.

Their red bushy tail does have a white tip on it. The babies muzzle will get longer and quite pointed. They will have large pointed ears that have black tips on them. The foxes lower legs are black and, all in all, an adult fox is a handsome animal, especially when seen on a background of fresh, white snow.

In a few minutes, baby fox number four is born. This baby lies very still. The mother picked it up with her mouth and put it by her mouth. Mother fox began licking this reluctant baby and shortly it began to make high pitched squeaks. Mother fox continued licking and directing this newborn baby to its private nipple. With its mouth full, the baby stopped making the high-pitched squeaking sounds.

Finally, the fifth kit is born. This is the biggest of the litter so far. It also had the biggest voice and mother fox quickly picks it up and begins licking it off and directing this pup to its own nipple. Mother fox knows that any loud excessive noise could attract animals or man to come looking for this source of sound. In time, mother fox has licked all of her babies and they all have filled their bellies with warm rich milk and now they were all sound asleep.

Mother fox is exhausted so she sleeps too. She wakes and checks her babies and find they are all there and appear to be alright. She gives each one a lick and about then father fox brings two recently caught mice and presents them to mother fox. She happily eats the meal brought to her.

Day by day the kits get bigger and explore more. The den

has very small space but now and then a baby tries to leave the nest. Mother fox picks it up and returns it to the nest.

By the end of April, the babies are much larger. They are allowed to come to the opening of the den. Their eyes are opened and are not as blue-gray as they were. The pups play 'rough and tumble' but at the first sign of danger, mother fox sends the babies back down the den. However, each day the pups explore more and more. They watch mother fox when she eats mice brought by father fox. They watch with more and more interest and two or three actually smell the mouse and try to get some away from their mother.

By the middle of June, these kits are about half-grown. Their legs are nearly as large as they will be. Their coats are nice and red. They can run very fast and when they are not sleeping, they are exploring or rough housing. Father fox brought dead mice and presented them to the pups. At first they smelled the mouse, pawed it with their front foot and eventually picked it up. The other pups tried to get the mouse from who has it in its mouth. They couldn't figure out that the mouse was good to eat.

By the end of June, the pups knew how to eat mice and when father fox brought live mice and presented them to the pups, they knew what to do. By now all five pups knew what to do with the mouse and they regularly ate them.

These half grown pups were very adventuresome. Mother fox had warned them about the railroad, the highway, the man that lived on the hill and dogs that roamed free. All the pups did not listen to their mother as well as they should. Mother fox would give the offending young fox a nip on its back with her sharp teeth. This bite didn't bring blood but the young fox got the message. That didn't mean that the young fox wouldn't do the same thing again.

Day by day, the young foxes roamed farther away from the den. Most of the time all five young fox stayed together as they explored. They were fascinated by the small stream that flowed near the den. They tried catching the frogs that lived there and had no luck as the frogs were too quick. Anyone watching these young fox trying to catch frogs would get a laugh out of their actions. Ears perked up and very attentive, the pack would surround the frog and finally one of the foxes would pounce and try to catch the frog. The frog hopped and immediately the other foxes were right after it. They might try to catch the frog in the air but most times they missed. Eventually, the frog disappeared under water and the pack moved on.

Small pools contained brook trout and these really frustrated the pups. Ears up and alert, noses pointed toward the water, the pups would pounce into the water trying to pin a trout down with its feet. The water would fly but the pups were never able to catch a trout in the pool. Once in awhile, the pups would chase a trout out of the pool and the escaping trout had to swim in some shallow water on its way to another pool. This action caused an immediate reaction by the pups. One day, one of the pups caught a trout as it swam in shallow water. The squirming trout got away from the fox but was grabbed by another pup before it could swim away. The fox with the trout, immediately ran away with the squirming trout. The rest of the pack was in hot pursuit and after a short chase, the fox with the trout stopped and the pack tried to get the trout. Eventually, the trout got eaten and every pup got some of it. All this activity required all five to lie down in a heap and sleep.

There was a farm on a hill not far from the den. Lots of sounds came from the farm. Cows and calves bellowing, dogs barking and machines running. Smells came from the farm also. One smell was coming from a pen of young chickens. One day the scent of those chickens was too much for the pups. They had to find out what that smell was. The pack simply followed the scent and walked right up to the chicken pen. This action caused the half-grown chickens to make a commotion when they saw these fox pups outside the chicken wire fence.

The pups went around to the other side of the pen because that is where the chickens ran to get away from the fox. This action caused the fox pack to go to the opposite side of the pen. The owner of the chickens heard all the commotion and came to investigate. He saw the fox pups and went back into the house to get a gun. The fox pups saw the man coming and they started running away. The sound of the shotgun really scared the pups but two of the pups got hit by the shotgun pellets. The pups that were hit immediately let out a yelp. One pup was hit in its hind leg by two pellets. That pup could not use that leg but it held it up and ran as fast as the others. The other pup that was hit had three pellets in its body. One in the back, one in the neck and one in its right front foot. It was not able to run as fast as the rest of the pack but they were out of range of the shotgun.

When the pack got back to the den, mother fox was very upset. She smelled the injured fox and gave each of the pups a hard bite to let them know that they should not have gone after the chickens. The two injured pups began licking the places where the pellets went in. Mother fox knew that the man with the gun may come looking for the five pups. She knew that this fox family must move to another den. She already knew where it was so she called the pups and they followed her for about one mile to a new den, but one that mother fox used last year. By now the pups didn't spend much time in the den, but it was still home to the foxes.

The two injured pups didn't feel good. They licked the wounds and it helped but the pup with the pellets in its back and neck became listless. Mother fox licked on it and nudged the pup with her nose. Eventually the pup died but mother fox kept licking it and lying close to her baby. The other wounded pup walked with a limp but it survived. The pack of pups was staying close to the den as the pups seemed to have learned a lesson after what happened with the chickens and the shotgun.

This new den was close to a highway and mother fox was worried that her pups would not be careful around the highway. There were many mice near this new den. The pups were slowly learning to catch mice by listening for their squeaks. Pouncing on the mouse with its feet and then using its mouth to catch the mouse. Another favorite food for fox is rabbit and the rabbits were plentiful in this area of the new den. Catching a rabbit was far different than catching a mouse. Rabbits run very fast but mother fox shows the pups how to catch rabbits. Most times it means a hard chase but one rabbit is equal to many mice.

The pups found a rabbit and were chasing it and it ran across the highway with two pups in hot pursuit. A car was moving fast on the highway and the rabbit made it across alright but one of the pups was hit by the car. It's right hind leg was broken but the pup was able to get back to the den. Mother fox licked the injured leg and, in time, the bone healed but that pup had a distinctive limp.

By mid-summer, the four pups were nearly full grown. They

were very curious and if they saw people in the woods they would approach them. Mother fox had warned them about people. Also by now, the pups went their own way by themselves.

One pup remembered the smell of chickens and since it had not been hit by any shotgun pellets, it had no bad memory of going to the farm on the hill. The pup could hear the chickens and he approached from   downwind. Eventually, he arrived at the pen where the chickens were kept. They were much larger now and two of them were outside of the pen. The pup carefully sneaked up by staying in some tall grass. At the proper time, the pup charged out and grabbed a chicken. This chicken, along with all the rest, made a tremendous commotion. This alerted the man who owned the chickens so he took his shotgun and ran to the chicken pen. The pup was struggling with the chicken as it was larger than any other prey it had grabbed. Besides that, the chicken was beating on the pup with its wings. The pup tried to drag the chicken into the tall grass which also impeded the fox.

The man with the shotgun saw the fox attempting to steal the chicken. He was in range but did not want to shoot at the fox because his pellets would also hit the chicken, which was very much alive. He shouted at the fox and it immediately let go of the chicken. The fox quickly ran straight away but after about two jumps, it made a hard turn toward the right. About then the man fired his shotgun and shot off more than half of the pups long bushy red tail with the white tip on the end. The chicken appeared to be alright and the pup had rapid speed as it sought the shelter of the woods.

The pup sought out the mother fox and she licked and licked on the stub of a tail that was left. The pup also got several sharp nips on its back. That pup looked strange without its full length tail streaming out behind as it ran.

On a dirt road near the den, mother fox found a trap that someone had set to catch foxes, coyotes and maybe raccoons. Mother fox brought all four pups to the trap and showed them where it was. She then dug it out as it was set in a bank beside the road. There was a piece of meat buried behind the trap and when an animal went to dig the meat out, they would get a foot caught in the trap. After the pups had seen the trap, Mother fox scratched great amounts of dirt, leaves and grass over the trap. She then went to each pup and nipped it on the back. Two pups yelped when nipped.

By fall, the pups had left their mother and had begun searching for their own territory. Mother fox had actually chased the pups away. Mother fox hated to do this but she knew the territory that mother and father fox had could not support any more fox except when they are babies.

Baby Crows

There are always crows around. Apparently crows exist all over the world. Around northwest Wisconsin there are many, many crows. One mother crow had laid five blue-green eggs, a little smaller than hens eggs, in a nest near the top of a good sized basswood tree. The nest is made out of twigs and grass and is about one and one-half feet in diameter. The eggs are laid in March and the mother crow sets on them until they hatch, toward the end of April. The parents bring food to these fledglings and they grow rapidly. Crows are scavengers and prefer to eat dead animals and that is what the baby crows get to eat most of the time. Crows will eat a variety of things. They seek out insects, various seeds, small rodents like mice, gophers shrews and chipmunks.

The baby crows grow rapidly and in about three to four weeks they are standing on the edge of their nest, flapping their wings in preparation to flying out of the nest. By now, the five young crows have grown so much that they are about to push each other out of the nest. One day, they begin to crow. Well, it is being made by a crow but is really a deep throated squawk and it is loud. About this time, either because they were pushed or wanted to fly on their own the young crows leave the nest and fly to a nearby tree. The flight is shaky and wobbly and when attempting to land on a branch, many attempts fail and the baby crow continues on and tries to land. Some attempts end up on the ground as some babies continue to lose altitude as they fly and some can't seem to be able to land on a branch.

Mother and father crow attend to these young crows. Perching next to them and 'cawing' loudly, they apparently are telling these young crows the facts of life. The parents continue to bring food to their loud-mouth offspring. The babies waste no time in letting the world know that they need food and lots of it! Their deep-pitched squawk is almost objectionable, but for anyone hearing it, they realize these are young crows crying out much like small human babies.

In a few days, their flying ability is much improved. They fly from limb to limb on the same tree. Later they fly to a nearby tree and with mother and father crows constant 'cawing'. A few days later in mid-June these babies can fly very well and go with their parents in search of dead animals or other food. Crows have excellent vision and farmers out cutting hay may kill a mouse and the crow flying overhead will spot that dead mouse, fly down, pick it up and fly away with it. The eagle is proclaimed to have excellent sight but I think the crow is equally well-sighted.

Kids have tried hard to shoot these crows. If you live in the country, many townships have a twenty-five cent bounty on each crow. The trick is that in order to collect this huge sum of money, the hunter has to present a crows head to the person who pays out bounties, usually the town clerk. It may sound easy, but crows are wary, super wary and if you leave your house intending to hunt crows and get rich on the bounty, these rascals will see you when you are a few feet from your house and sound the alarm, if you are carrying a gun. You have no chance as the word spreads like wildfire, watch out for this guy! If you hold the gun by your side and leg, do not bother, these rascals see right through that and spread the word. On the other hand, if you just walk out of your house and toward the woods, with no gun, there won't even be a peep out of the crows. Anyone hoping to sneak up on crows in order to shoot them, better think again.

Crows always have spies that keep an eye out for any suspicious activity. When justified, the message goes out to every crow within miles to be alert because there is danger in the kingdom.

Besides man, the crows bitter enemies are owls and hawks. Apparently, owls come to where the crows are roosting for the night and kill a crow. They probably take it to their roost and eat it. Because it is dark, the crows can't follow the owl as the owl can see very well in very dim light. The next day or two, the crows find the offending owl and call in every crow within miles. Their intention is to harass the owl and if they have enough courage, they will kill it.

This means that there are a hundred or more crows, all squawking at the top of their lungs at the owl. Anyone within a couple miles will hear this racket and wonder what is going on.

By mid-summer, the baby crows are full grown and are good fliers. The babies are very curious and sometimes will come in around people but mother crow lets them know, with a crows tongue lashing, don't do that again! Crows seem very smart and an old story I read once, told about a crow that was thirsty and saw a water pitcher with water in the bottom. The crow could not reach the water but it picked up rocks and dropped them into the pitcher and the water rose enough for the crow to get a drink. Pretty clever.

It doesn't take long to figure out why there is a bounty on crows. They pull up garden and field plants, their constant 'cawing' is a distraction but many of us admire these large black birds. Any animal killed on the road is a meal, or many meals, for crows. They are good at judging the speed and distance a vehicle is from where they are munching on road kill. Some are so brazen that they don't even fly when a car goes past in the other lane.

Crows have been captured when they were very young and they have become pets. They are very curious and watch all the comings and goings on around anyone's home. They have been known to pick up small shiny things and carry them off and hide them. These tame crows apparently have a good sense of humor as they have been known to fly down and peck at the tail of a cat. They may try to get food a cat is carrying by pulling its tail. Crows can talk, or at least one crow can. At a zoo in Chippewa Falls, Wisconsin, there was a crow by the name of Jimmy and the sign said he could talk. I heard Jimmy say 'Hello' three different times. I don't know if he could say any other words.

Baby Killdeer

The killdeer is one of the first birds to return to northwest Wisconsin in the spring. They are fairly small ground birds that are smaller than robins. They have a loud, nearly continual song which they keep singing well into the night on some nights. They make a nest in a naturally, slightly rounded, indentation in the ground. Mother killdeer quite often lay three to five eggs. This takes a week or more for all of the eggs to finally be laid. These eggs seem large for the size of mother killdeer. The eggs are light tan in color with brown spots on them. The small end of all the eggs meet in the center of the nest.

Both killdeer parents share the chore of setting on the nest. The nest is located in strange places. It may be in the lawn, along a busy highway, in pastures or in barnyards very near buildings. The birds are brown on their back but there are two white throat bands that aid in their being very difficult to see when sitting on their nest.

It takes a long time to incubate the eggs, approximately three to four weeks. If animals or people come too close to the nest, one or both parents put up a tremendous squawking and drop one wing and fan it out and pretend that it is broken. They want to lure the object of this commotion away from the nest. If a person follows this 'injured' bird and gets far enough away from the nest, the bird suddenly heals up and flies away. A friend of mine told me that there was a killdeer nest in the pasture that the cows and calves were in. Some calves discovered the mother or father setting on the eggs and came closer and closer to the nest. The bird on the nest finally left the nest, flared out her wings and tail feathers and began snapping her beak as he or she shrilly objected to the calves coming close to the nest. Finally, the bird had to jump up and snap the calf in the nose with its beak. Eventually the calves continued on their way and in a couple days the eggs hatched into little balls of fluff with feet. After they are dried off, these little balls of soft fluff can really run. If they stop, they blend into the surroundings.

One of my classmates told me that he was walking along the shore of a very small lake when all of a sudden five baby killdeer ran out from under their mothers outstretched wings. Three of them immediately ran into the lake and swam about one hundred feet to the shore in a different part of the lake. The other two simply ran under some grass and stopped there. My friend backed off a distance and sat down. Mother killdeer had flown over to where the three swimmers had come to shore. She began to urge them to follow her back to the other two chicks. Within an hour, mother killdeer had reunited all five of her chicks and all was good.

That same friend said that every summer lately there are from two to five killdeer nests by his place. By the end of May or *into June, these little babies have hatched and are able to run like crazy. They are so small that you could easily hold one in your hand with your fingers closed, in the first few days after hatching. These babies eat lots of insects and their song is very pleasant and pleasing to hear. Sometimes, a pair will raise two sets of chicks in a summer. Quite often, killdeer are among the last birds to fly south for the winter.*

Early Wednesday, December 28, 1948

Today, Mom, Dad and I go to Savannah's cabin. Not knowing what is planned, Dad is taking some ice fishing gear and I am taking our Alaskan snowshoes. These are about four feet long and about one foot wide and in this deep snow, it will be hard to walk with them, but nearly impossible to walk without snowshoes.

Late Wednesday, December 28, 1948

Wow! This was an exciting day. We arrived at the cabin by 9:30 a.m. Elon and Kathy had coffee and sweet rolls waiting for us. An hour was spent talking about various things but the strike by the coal miners was beginning to be a big worry for both families as both homes were heated with coal. Both Mom and Kathy hated the black, sooty grime that was in evidence in both houses. It was a never ending job to clean up this black grime that seemed to be on everything in the house. Spooner's nickname was 'The Smoke Hole', mostly from all the steam locomotives that burned coal. Even though there are very few steamers running, the nickname seems to persist. Our coal burning furnace produces some black smoke and snow doesn't stay snow white very long.

The day was very pleasant. There was blue sky, with the temperature about 30° F. and very little wind. One thing I wanted to do was go to the old house, go upstairs and see what made the loud clunk. Savannah said she had a pair of snowshoes and she also wanted to go to the old house, somewhat reluctantly. We told our folks we were going for a snowshoe walk.

We got the snowshoes and walked to the end of the driveway and put the snowshoes on. Ready to go, I led the way as we had to get up and over the huge snow bank pushed up by the snowplow. Dad showed me how to do this last year by walking up to the bank, parallel to it and begin to sidestep your way up the bank. Sometimes it took some kicking your snowshoe in order to make a little ledge to stand on. It didn't take very long and we were over the bank and in deep snow. Even with snowshoes, I sank in about a foot. After a few hundred feet I had to rest. Not only do you sink in but you need to bring your foot out of the deep hole so this awkward motion is tiring. While we were resting, I told Savannah what I suspected about her dad making the noise that scared us all so bad. She definitely thought her dad was capable of doing something like that as he was a prankster. She secretly wondered if her dad had been responsible for the noise. After all, he was supposed to be helping Grandpa but you and I don't know that he was.

We approached the old house, now weighted down with a thick blanket of snow. We saw where part of the roof of the porch had collapsed and we were concerned. Maybe the old house might collapse under the weight of all this snow. We stood by the porch steps and discussed the possibility of the entire house going down. Finally, we decided that I would go upstairs and see if I could determine anything.

I took my snowshoes off and cautiously started up the porch steps. I told Savannah, "I am not too brave about doing this, but here goes." I opened the front door and walked in. I looked around and listened. No strange sounds so I began to go up the stairs to the bedrooms. I slowly went up the stairs and when I was near the top, there was a loud thump from one of the bedrooms. Not only that, there was the sound of laughter, like ha-ha-ha-ha! Needless to say, I turned around and took the steps, three at a time and ran out on the porch and jumped off. Savannah still had her snowshoes on and I nearly knocked her over.

I finally calmed down, and thanks to urging from Savannah, we moved off a few feet and talked about what I had heard. Savannah asked, "Did you hear any other sounds besides the thump and the four ha-ha's?" I said, "No, now that you mention it." I was silent for a few minutes and finally a thought crossed my mind. "When we were here with the three girls and we were on our way up the stairs, I was on about the same step when we heard the big thump. I wonder

146

if something is rigged to trip if someone steps on that particular step?"

Savannah wondered, "If we go back into the house and walk up the stairs, we could see if another thump occurs. Maybe the laughing sound is caused when someone steps on that certain step." After a long pause, I said, "Are you game to go back in the house and walk up the stairs to see if anything happens?" Savannah gave me a look of dismay, but then said, "Let's go."

We did not exactly charge up the stairs, but we slowly moved, step by step, until I got to the step where I heard the noises. There was no sound other than the sound of my beating heart in my ears. I looked back at Savannah and I could tell she was not enjoying this very much. I continued up the stairs and in a few steps I was off the stair steps and headed for the closed door that the sound came from. Savannah was right behind me and grabbed my arm and whispered, "Are you going to open the door?" I asked her, "Do you prefer that I didn't?" There was a long pause and she said, "I am scared, but I think we both want to know what is behind that door."

I grasped the door knob and turned it, half expecting something to jump out at us. I pushed the door open and nothing sprang out at us. I pushed the door open so we could see the entire room, except what was behind the door.

As we looked in the room, we could see it might have been a bedroom, but there was no furniture at all. However, there was a small log laying on the floor. It was about four feet tall and about seven or eight inches in diameter. There was a wire attached to one end of the log. The wire went up to a hook in the closet. The wire went down to the juncture of the floor and wall, then passed through a hole there. I was pretty sure I knew where it went so I went down the stairs to the step I was on when the thump occurred. Sure enough, the wire came through the hole, hung down and did not go to the step as I thought it would. Then I realized that when the log fell it pulled at least four feet of wire with it. I went back upstairs and explained what I thought happened.

We set the log up and it was cut on an angle so it leaned when we put it upright. I took the slack out of the wire, pushed it down the hole and went down and pulled up the slack. The wire then reached the step in question. I looked at the end of the step and could see that if the wire was pushed into a small hole, the wire stayed in place. I went up the stairs and stepped on the step in question and immediately the wire released and the log fell over with a thump. About a minute later, I heard ha-ha-ha-ha and then Savannah's laughter. I went up stairs and found Savannah holding a bell-shaped object, about three inches in diameter with a small thin rope passing through it from top to bottom. Savannah showed me how it worked. There were four small knots on this thin rope which hung from a hook in a corner of the room.

Savannah slid the bell-shaped object up the string going over the four knots, one at a time. When she let the bell thing drop, it let out a 'ha' each time it went over a knot. Savannah said she noticed this thin thread attached to the log laying on the floor. It lead into this corner and had a small pin attached to it. I looked at the bell and, sure enough, there was a place to put the pin and that would hold the bell up on its thin rope until the pin was pulled by the log falling over.

We looked at each other and had a big laugh. We hugged each other and had a long, passionate kiss. Savannah certainly is a good kisser but I have no one to compare her to. I don't see how a kiss could be any more exciting and pleasant than the kisses I get from Savannah.

We decided to reset the log and the wire so someone else could get scared like we were. We talked about who could have done this and Savannah said it had her dad written all over it. We decided to look in the other room, so we carefully opened the door and started to go in when, all at once, there was a huge crash and something fairly large and furry came flying up off the floor right at us. We both screamed and turned and ran into the other room.

This was almost too much. We cautiously looked toward the room we just left. There, hanging in the doorway, was the skin of a raccoon over a wadded up towel. Whew. At least it was not a real animal. We went back and stepped through the door and looked behind the door. We saw a 2 x 4 about five feet tall. It had a stand built to keep it from tipping over. Laying at the base of the 2 x 4 was a good sized chunk of firewood with a wire attached to it that ran to a hook nearly over the door opening we were going to step through. We put the block of wood up on the 2 x 4 and positioned it so that the door would hit it and knock it off. We then positioned the fake raccoon about where it seemed to come from. We pushed the firewood off the 2 x 4 and in a flash, the raccoon skin jumped up right about face level. Once again, we had a huge laugh. We reset the firewood and the raccoon so it could continue scaring folks.

We looked around the room and thought it was another bedroom. There was a door possibly to a storage area. We decided not to open that door and headed back downstairs. Savannah said, "We definitely are not going to open the trap door in the floor." I agreed. We hugged and kissed and then went outside and put on our snowshoes and headed back to the cabin. On the way, I told Savannah, "I received a call from Earl and he sounded great. Things are going fine at school and Margaret has helped him with updating his study skills." Savannah said, "Margaret called a couple days ago. Earl is remodeling the bathroom over Christmas break. They do plan to come to the cabin for New Years Eve."

When we got back to the cabin, I got the gift for Savannah out of the car. She said she had a gift for me, too. Savannah opened the copper bracelet and said she loved it and put it on. I opened the gift to me and it was a beautiful silver identification bracelet with **NICK 1948** engraved on it. It was really nice. I told her the bracelet was wonderful. We had a nice lunch and visited with our mom's while we ate. We told them about what we discovered at the old house. They both acted like they didn't know anything about who might have done it. Kathy immediately thought it was her brother, the 'Brush Cop'. She said he was always doing tricks like that when they were kids. I am still thinking it was Savannah's dad. Maybe we will never know.

After lunch, Savannah and I went for a walk on the road. We held hands and talked about lots of things. I told her that I had written a possible story called *The Mob and the Deer Hunter.* She wanted to hear the story so I told her and she was amazed at my creativity. She said she really liked the story and hoped to see it in a book someday. I told her it would be a small book, but maybe. I then told her about the three possible stories for kids. She was fascinated by all three stories about the foxes, the crows and the killdeer. She said she loves baby animals and enjoys seeing them or reading about them. She wanted to know if I was going to write about any other wild babies. I said I was thinking about it but hadn't decided what other animals to write about yet. She suggested baby otters. I told her I had thought about the saw-whet owl babies that I saw this summer or maybe baby beavers. The problem is I really don't know much about these animals.

By this time, the afternoon was nearly done and Dad and Elon were returning from ice fishing. They had about two dozen really nice bluegills. While fishing for these pan fish, they put out a rig called a 'tip-up'. They each used one and they were Elon's. He just got them and they showed them to us. There is a little wooden frame that is put over the hole. There is a small reel with line on it and it is in the water. A minnow is put on a hook and when the proper depth is reached, the little spring loaded flag on top is set so that if a fish bites the minnow, the line goes out and a little knob on the reel flies the flag up and the fisherman knows something grabbed the bait. Today they had two tip-ups go up but they didn't catch anything.

Savannah and I filleted the bluegills and Kathy started frying them. Mom had made a nice salad and we ate that along with some fried potatoes and the wonderful fish. This was a meal fit for a king. All of us were stuffed but Kathy brought out a pecan pie and we all ate a piece of this wonderful pie. The dishes were washed and it was time for us to head home as Dad had to drive a train early tomorrow. It was a wonderful day. Savannah and I hugged and kissed and said goodbye.

Early Thursday, December 29, 1948

The gym is open this afternoon from 1:00 to 4:00 p.m. and I will go and shoot baskets and maybe get in a basketball game. I decided to write about more wild babies.

Baby Deer

About the middle of May, in northwest Wisconsin, a doe deer gives birth to a fawn and after licking it off she delivers another fawn. It gets licked and, in a few minutes, it gets up on its wobbly legs. Both fawns are very small, about the size of a small cat, but they have long legs and white spots on their brown coats. They have a black nose, black eyes and big, alert ears. Their short tail is white on the underside, just like their mothers.

These newborns are hungry and, with a little coaxing from their mother, they locate her udder between her hind legs. There is a nipple on each side of the udder and these fawns find one for each of them and begin to suckle. The mother turns her head around and licks the fawns as they drink her warm, rich milk. Only an hour or two old, these fawns wiggle their tail as they drink.

After drinking their fill, the mother directs them to a spot in some ferns where they lie down with their head over their hind legs. They will stay in that spot for many hours until the mother comes back and gets them up. The mother spends much time away from the fawns eating. Not being near her babies is a critical time, as there are coyotes, timber wolves and bears that will kill and eat these young fawns.

Day by day, the babies get larger and stronger and nearly every time after suckling, the two babies rough house by bunting each other, running around and playing fawn tag. When mother gives the sign the babies find a sheltered spot and lie down. Day by day, the fawns grow more bold and get scolded by their mother. She may give them a gentle whack with one of her front feet. She may also nip their back and shoulder. One way or another, the fawns get the message 'behave yourselves'.

They also can jump nearly as high as their mother over dead falls, fences, streams or other things. By the end of summer, the fawns are beginning to turn darker but still have their spots. They are approaching two-thirds of their mothers size and by now are becoming more self-sufficient at finding food. They still suckle from their mother but she will soon kick them away as she wants to wean them. Part of the reason is that she is about to begin the mating season so new fawns will be formed. The two fawns will follow their mother and she will look after them, but she will not let them nurse.

Mother deer has warned the fawns about many dangers, one of which is the road. One day in June she approached a road with her babies following her. There was a big hill on this road and she was going to cross about halfway down the hill. She cautiously crosses and the two fawns were about to step on the road when, all *at once, a car came over the hill. The mother signaled her fawns to 'stop and lie down' and they did. On the edge of the road, these two very young fawns squatted down as low as they could. The driver had seen the mother and the two fawns so he stopped and shut his car off. The mother was very nervous but the fawns would not move. Finally, the mother deer walked back to where the fawns were and gave the signal to follow her and they all ran back the way they had come.*

By October, one of the fawns started to develop some nubs of antlers. This one is a buck fawn and by the end of November this little buck will be called a 'nubbin buck' or a 'button buck'. If he survives until next spring he will grow his first set of antlers. He could live several years and for the first four or five years, his antlers will be the biggest of his life. Getting the proper mineral is a big factor, too.

The other fawn is a young doe and, in November she will get the urge to mate and, by next May she may have fawns of her own. For both fawns, there still is deer season ahead of them and this year they should be protected as a legal deer has to have a forked horn. There are people that shoot any deer, legal or not. If they survive the deer season, the deep snows of winter may kill them as they starve to death. The deer is a much admired, sleek, graceful, alert and beautiful animal but, when herds of them are in a field eating crops or young trees, we realize that everything about the deer may not be good.

Baby Otters

These weasel family members live in rivers or streams and are born in the spring in a burrow in a bank of a river or stream. They suckle on their mother and in a few weeks both mother and father otter bring small amounts of fish back to the pups. These animals have fine, dark fur and are valued for their fur. They have a fairly broad, inquiring face and are excellent swimmers being able to catch fish, including trout.

The otter is mother natures happy troubadour and is constantly poking its nose into anything that looks like it needs exploring. Otters like to slide down riverbanks, snow-covered banks

152

and appear very well equipped for doing this as they are long and sleek and tuck their feet under them when they slide.

By early summer, these pups venture out of the burrow and are watched carefully by both otter parents. Families may have several babies in them. They are very acrobatic and constantly play with their brothers and sisters. By late summer, the family is still together and by now the babies are nearly as large as their parents. They also are able to catch fish and other food like frogs, crayfish and maybe a clam.

'Rough' told of going down a small river in a canoe with his dad hunting ducks. All at once, they were surrounded by about seven otters. They were quite close to the canoe and would poke their head out of the water to watch them. All at once, they let out a 'muffled woof' and would disappear. For several minutes these otters kept spying on 'Rough' and his father. Eventually the canoe moved down stream and this family followed for a few hundred feet and then apparently went back upstream.

I heard of a family in eastern Wisconsin that somehow had obtained two young otters. They were wonderful, happy animals and the family loved them. The family let their otters play in the bathtub and, to begin with, that was fine. As they got larger, so did the splashes of water. Watching these two play was apparently a very funny event.

One day the family locked the half-grown otters in their cage which was in the house. The family returned after about three hours. They opened the door to the house which opened into the kitchen - **total disaster.** The otters had managed to get out of their cage and proceeded to empty all the cupboards, shelves, drawers and counter tops. Flour and corn meal was everywhere. Somehow they had not found a way to get the refrigerator open, but they had tried. Their hand prints reached to within a few inches of the refrigerator door latch.

These happy go lucky otters were happy to see the family and came to them and jumped up to be cradled and petted. They were covered with water soaked flour and cornmeal. They had figured out how to get the water faucet turned on and luckily only a small stream of water was flowing.

The family was very upset but they had no intention of

punishing the otters. They did get returned to their cage and were cleaned up later. Immediately a phone call was made to a zoo that had heard about these playful rascals and they would take them. The kitchen was cleaned, new dishes purchased as well as a wide variety of provisions. The zoo folks came for the two otters and it was a very sad time for the family, but they realized that these amazing, loving animals had to leave their home. They remarked that their experience was similar to what happened in the story of 'The Yearling'. At least the family didn't have to take the life of the otters.

Early Friday, December 30, 1948

There is open gym this afternoon and I will go. I will meet my buddies there and we will be able to play against some of the varsity players. Jim, Jed, and Joe will all be there but they have things to do this morning so we will meet this afternoon.

Late Friday, December 30, 1948

Things got pretty rough under the boards, but we held our own. 'Rough', 'Tough', Joe and I are all pretty husky and we all like to mix it up with physical contact. It was great working with the varsity guys.

I will write in my diary as I have some thoughts I want to put down on paper.

I can't get Beaver Brook, the brook, out of my mind. This moving body of water starts out quite small and gets larger. Everybody starts out as a baby and we are very dependent on our moms and dads for many months. Baby animals, in many cases, have to be able to get up and get moving minutes after their birth, either from being born or hatching. The fawns and killdeer chicks get going in minutes. The fox pups, baby crows and baby otters all need lots of care. In a few months, all the animal babies are on their own. We, on the other hand, need help for many months. We need to learn to walk, talk and other activities. These activities are learned at different rates. We have a much longer lifetime and maybe by percentage of each of our lives spent before we are independent compared to our length of life may be all about the same.

This brook begins small and water from many springs makes it gradually larger. That is like any baby human or wild animal. We not only get larger, we learn to do many new skills. Help learning these skills is mostly by the parents. Many times rough and tumble play by baby animals is actually learning survival skills, hunting skills and social skills. My mom and dad were the biggest help to me in learning to talk, crawl, walk, stand up and eventually run. The brook got larger as more springs fed water to it.

Eventually, baby animals become self-sufficient but may still be part of a group, flock or pack. The foxes stayed near each other for many months but then the parents drive them away to find their own territory. The crows apparently stay in the same family structure. The killdeer appear to stay with the family group but many get dispersed when they leave in the fall. The fawns learn from their mother and apparently they winter the first winter with mother deer. The baby otters stay with their mother and father at least through winter and then they are dispersed to find their own territory. Young beavers and muskrats are reported wandering far from water apparently driven out of the territory they were born in. Timber wolf packs are well known for driving out certain young wolves so they must find their own territory.

I don't think I will ever be driven out of Mom and Dad's home. I very likely will leave and eventually establish my own home. I may live near home, or I may even work with my mom or dad, quite unlike the animal babies talked about.

As I think about the brook, I saw two fairly large streams of water join with the brook. Maybe the first stream, coming under the railroad trestle, is when I met Savannah! The brook got larger as did my development with this beautiful, friendly, wonderful girl. The brook is now larger and more complex. I now had to develop my skills about getting along with a girl that I really liked and respected. I had no particular training but my life with my mom and dad served me well - up to a point. I needed help from my brook as I tried to understand Savannah and her parents. I wanted to be Savannah's friend and I wanted her to like me as much as I liked her.

My brook got slightly larger as did my perspective on how to treat Savannah with all the respect that I felt she deserved. I hoped I could be a good friend to her as we developed our own relationship with each other. Coming into my brook is Savannah's parents and my parents. I was submissive to my parents as I loved and respected them and their love for me. An underlying feeling was beginning to challenge their love. I wanted approval, maybe more from Savannah's mom and dad also.

My brook kept flowing on and one day Earl enters the picture. By now my brook had become larger and maybe I could deal with Earl and all of the war tragedy that had happened to him. By now the brook was flowing by my campsite. If there was a magical spot for me in my fifteen years it was that beautiful campsite under the grove of tall white pines. Looking back at that campsite, it was a place for me to seek out my feelings, learn to respect others, especially Savannah and later, Earl. Coming to grips with my own fear of sounds in the night and wondering if I could sleep in my tent, prepare meals and take care of day to day tasks without feeling like I wanted to go home.

The brook keeps flowing and getting larger. I was able to be a good friend to Earl and when he got lost, I was able to find him and be a strong leader for him. Kathy and Elon were very supportive. When Margaret fell in the brook and got injured, I was able to come to her aid. The brook flowed on and I was able to help Margaret get to a doctor and that required a great effort from both of us.

I was amazed that I could take off and explore the huge forest, the cranberry marsh and meet Little Dove and Walking Bear. The brook flows on. It gets larger. Finding Joe Pachoes den, the trappers cabin, the old logging camp and the hunters cabin were amazing discoveries that I am proud of. I really am amazed that I had the courage to do all of these things in this huge forest. The brook gets larger as it flows along.

I felt that I was not the same fourteen-year-old boy that set up his tent at the beginning of the summer. The magic of the brook gave me strength when I was afraid in the night. Maybe the brook was my mother in abstention.

If I had not gotten courage from the brook, I would not have met Dick and Joe or Jerry and Pete. The sluice dam timbers really made me think. These were placed by men at least fifty years ago. For what reason? The brook taught me about being patient, answers are not always obvious. In fact, some answers are not possible to find.

Just upstream of the sluice dam is the large stream of very cold water coming into the Beaver. For some reason, I am now getting a feeling about this stream as relating to my camping near the brook. It was a significant player in my relationship with Savannah, Earl, Dick and Joe.

Many hours passed and suddenly it hit me. The stream coming from the beaver pond represented the news that I was adopted! That was a shocker and that stream was the largest addition to the brook. Finding out about my birth mother, Jean, very near death, and learning that I had a younger brother, a younger sister and a birth father just about took me down. My mom and dad, with me from the time the brook started to flow, stood by me and gave me the support to meet Jean and listen to her tell why she had to give me up for adoption. The brook flowed on and was full of water. I needed all the brook could give me to understand all that was around me. I felt great love from a dying birth mother who needed to see me before she passed away.

To my mom and dad who had been the kindest, most loving parents any boy could have. The brook flowed on and now I needed strength to deal with this beautiful, friendly, kind lady that wanted to see her oldest son before she died. My heart was close to breaking but the cold water from the beaver pond made me stronger. With difficulty, I was able to realize I had two mothers, two fathers, a brother and a sister.

The brook flows on and I started school as a freshman. The brook is much larger by now and I have become a bigger, stronger boy, both physically and mentally. I am about the happiest boy in the world. *The Brook Flows On.*

EPILOG

Nick loves to write. Now, fifteen years old in 1948, this boy begins his freshman year at the Spooner, Wisconsin High School. He records many things in his diary and continues to interact with his tall, red-headed, trout fishing friend, Savannah. This is a long range friendship as Savannah lives in Antigo, Wisconsin, over one-hundred miles from Spooner.

Nick is still drawn to his old summer haunt, the Beaver Brook Wild Life Area. He constantly is reminded of his exciting summer, camping out and trout fishing on the beautiful stream called Beaver Brook.

Football season starts and young Nick is prepared after many hours practicing his 'Crazy Legs' drills at running in the woods, dodging trees and shifting the football (a piece of wood) from one hand to another. He is very fast and has an exciting football season.

Near the end of the football season, Nick receives some news that nearly takes him down. He relies on his mom and dad and day by day he gets through it.

Nick cannot get the desire to write a book out of his head. He includes his first story, in several parts, in his diary. He titled his story *The Mob and the Deer Hunter.* He also tried his hand at writing some children's stories called *Wild Animal Babies.*

Nick finally realizes that his life is like the brook he so admires. It starts small and gets larger as it flows along. *The Brook Flows On.*